MURDER MOVIE

Nobody had to tell George Kennedy that shooting a movie was hard work. But it wasn't the early calls, endless retakes, or life on location in Mexico that got to him. It was murder. One bizarre murder after another.

First the pretty script girl was sliced up like cold cuts. Then the stunt man missed his air bag at the bottom of the cliff.

With corpses coming in faster than film footage, Kennedy and cop-turned-actor Mike Corby had to figure everyone for a suspect—even stars Dean Martin, Glenn Ford, Raquel Welch, Genevieve Bujold, Mariette Hartley and Yul Brynner. With no clues, no motive, and death the only alibi, Kennedy and Corby had some fast acting to do. Or their final scene might be "exit dying."

MURDER ON LOCATION

GEORGE KENNEDY

AVON
PUBLISHERS OF BARD, CAMELOT, DISCUS AND FLARE BOOKS

MURDER ON LOCATION is an original publication of Avon Books. This work has never before appeared in book form.

AVON BOOKS
A division of
The Hearst Corporation
959 Eighth Avenue
New York, New York 10019

Copyright © 1983 by George Kennedy
Published by arrangement with the author
Library of Congress Catalog Card Number: 83-90625
ISBN: 0-380-83857-5

First Avon Printing, July, 1983

AVON TRADEMARK REG. U. S. PAT. OFF. AND IN OTHER COUNTRIES, MARCA REGISTRADA, HECHO EN U.S.A.

Printed in the U. S. A.

WFH   10 9 8 7 6 5 4 3 2 1

The real persons who appear in this book are not meant to resemble any fictional characters, living or dead. I have imagined certain celebrities as present in some of the scenes to add authenticity and a touch of glamor to the tale. They are all colleagues of mine for whom I have the highest regard. At any rate, they were never there, because, to tell the truth, none of this ever really happened except in my imagination, as I hope it will in yours as you read on.

GK

CHAPTER ONE

The day of the first murder began like any other day on location—early, before the sun was up.

A long procession of vehicles made its way toward the set, yellow headlights poking impudently into the darkest hour, which in Mexico really does come before the dawn.

There were buses, trucks, jeeps, and sedans, each reflecting a place in the pecking order, with, for example, stars like Glenn Ford and Raquel Welch in the sedans, and locally hired extras standing in the open truck beds, and those in-between riding in the various other vehicles.

Everyone, from actors to grips, from camera operators to gaffers, had consulted the call sheet the night before. This plan of the day was posted in the hotel lobby and also passed out to the rooms so that those who would be working in the scenes scheduled to be shot would be on hand. Scheduled to be shot if all went well.

Which it almost never did.

Before the skinny Mexican roosters were even thinking of crowing, all the people had piled into the vehicles, a few with fierce hangovers, most merely sleepy-eyed and grumpy. Dawn broke as we bounced over the dusty, rutted road. It was peach gray at first, blood red for a moment, and finally a glittering yellow, like Aztec gold.

I rode that morning with Lance Haverford, the producer, and Joel Totterelli, the director. That's right, Haverford and Totterelli. Nothing but the best for *The Godless,* which was a thirty-million-dollar production. A lot of money, you say? I say it, too, but the way things are in the motion-picture industry these days I say it almost without blinking. A project that costs, say, a lousy five million, for example, is, by present standards, a low-budget flick—a cheapie. Inflation has hit everywhere, I suppose, but nowhere as hard as in what we fondly call "the industry."

The three of us in the car didn't say much. Lance stared straight ahead with those burning eyes of his, and Joel, a smaller and quieter man, leaned back and yawned at intervals. They were a good team, these two, though they differed in everything from personal appearance to basic philosophy.

Lance Haverford, tall, lean, and bearded, looked as Satan must have looked when he was young.

Joel Totterelli, clean-shaven, slender, mild-eyed, was the nice guy next door who had a nice, steady job somewhere.

"I don't know if we'll make it to scene 82 today," Joel said to me.

"It's okay," I said. "I'll wait."

And wait I would, I knew. The saying in Hollywood is that an actor's two main requisites are a little talent and a lot of patience. As you probably know, the scenes are not scheduled in chronological order, but for efficiency of shooting, so that those on call spend their time on one set or in one area on a given day. Even so, there are many days when you simply hang around and never step in front of the camera.

When we arrived at the location area the caterers already had the breakfast fires burning in the big truck, and we lined up and gave our orders—for me, a bacon and egg sandwich with lots of onions. The onions were an indulgence; they unsettle my stomach, but I love them, and, what the hell, on location one tends to be a little reckless.

The sun, a burning medallion, rose higher and became hotter. The call, nearly every day in Mexico, was a "rain or shine" call, and could be, because it just about never rained.

After breakfast, I waited my turn to get costumed and made up in the honey wagon—a trailer with six individual dressing rooms—and when I emerged from that, in the guise of the drunken, eccentric town fire chief I was playing, they were already shooting Raquel Welch's ten-second walking scene at the well. I figured they'd be the rest of the morning on that. That was because Lance Haverford insisted on perfection, or, at any rate, his personal version of it. So, for that matter, did Joel Totterelli, though in a much quieter, less noticeable way.

I decided to stroll.

I headed for the big arroyo beyond the set, and that took me past the property van. Dean Martin, already made up as Carstairs, the unreconstructed Confederate renegade, was behind it, whacking at a line of balls with what looked like a nine-iron. One of them sailed high into the air, and when I looked again I saw that they weren't golf balls but horseturds.

I said, "Dean, what in hell are you doing?"

He grinned. "I'm not gettin' the same distance on my horseshit the way I used to!"

I laughed and moved on.

A little way out in the arroyo Mike Corby caught up with me.

"Quiet out here," said Mike, falling into step.

"Yeah," I said. That's enough dialogue for early morning.

"Not frantic, like back in Hollywood," said Mike.

I glanced at him. You probably know what Mike Corby looks like because, by now, he's had feature roles in several movies on both the tube and the big screen. Bulldog stocky, very tough, his nose a splayed-out "Z" splashed down the middle of his face. And those eyes. Cop's eyes. They go right through you and you can almost hear him thinking he's not *sure* you've done something wrong, but he'll just bet you have.

"Nice," he said, looking at the turquoise sky, "but it won't last forever. Gotta go back and face all that crap again sometime."

You remember *Badge of Honor*, which was based on Mike Corby's actual exploits in solving a string of sensational rape-murders back in New York City. "The Park Avenue Rapist," they called the nut who did it. I think the asshole's back on the street again.

Mike had been brought in as a technical advisor on the film, but they gave him a walk-on part, and, to their surprise, he looked pretty good. He almost stole the scene from Al Pacino, who, in the picture, was supposed to be Mike. Small parts in other dramas followed, and pretty soon they were in the habit of calling Mike whenever there was a tough cop to be cast in a minor role. In *The Godless*, for a switch, he was the town marshal.

"Look, Mike," I said, "I agree with you that it can get frantic at times, but, in all honesty now, and balancing the good against the bad, what's so terrible about it?"

"Maybe *you* don't find it lousy," he grumbled. "You were an actor from the start and you love it. The glamor, the excitement—"

I shook my head. "You've got it wrong, Mike. I like the work itself, not the glamor crap. I hardly even go to parties. I don't even table-hop."

He paused to kick a stone. Mike Corby, raised in the streets of New York and full of city smarts, a stone-kicker yet.

"George," he said, his brows going into dishrag folds, "since they made an actor out of me everything's been going wrong, you know what I mean?"

"No," I said. "I don't know what you mean. From where I stand, you've got it made. They want you. You do good work."

"Playing myself."

"You want to be Olivier or Brando or somebody? Do you realize how many people would poison their grandmothers just to be where you are?"

"Goddamnit, George," he said, "you don't know. Seems like all my troubles started since I got snuck through the back door and became an actor. The divorce, for a starter. Ellie thought she'd see more of me when we came out to Hollywood and wouldn't be a police widow anymore. But it was even worse. The way I always had to be somewhere, chasing around, meeting people, hassling with agents, setting up this deal and that. Kissing asses sometimes, in spite of myself. The parties. The dolls. What are you gonna do, for Christ's sake, when some gorgeous quiff, who wants something from you, is throwing it at you? Turn it down?"

"Some manage," I said.

He hardly heard me. "Then, young Dennis getting strung out. On hard stuff. It didn't get to him in P.S. 82, where you'd expect, but in Beverly Hills High, which is supposed to be high class!"

I shrugged. "We all have our troubles with the kids."

"The booze," he continued. "Before, maybe I'd reach for a drink once in a while at the end of a long day, but never just because I was sitting across from some schlock producer, who could make or break me, feeling ill at ease."

"So don't reach."

"And last, but not least," he said, "finances."

"What else is new?" I said. "Money is trouble, and it's here to stay."

"George, I don't know how it happened—the house, the cars, alimony, all the rest—but I now owe more than I make or probably ever will!"

"It's gotta be handled somehow," I said. Sometimes when you make noncommittal comments like this people think you've actually given them advice and feel better.

"Christ knows, I'm trying. *The Godless* will help, maybe. If it goes anywhere. Better parts, bigger prices. And then someday, down the road, I can pay off my obligations and settle down on campus where there's a little peace and quiet."

"Campus?"

"Guess I didn't tell you. I've got this master's degree from CCNY—that's how I made lieutenant. The University of New Mexico wants me as a resident in criminology. I always liked Albuquerque, even if it doesn't have a decent delicatessen."

"Then go that route," I said.

"I can't, the hole I'm in!" He straightened himself abruptly. "Hey—I'm sorry, George. I didn't mean to make a father-confessor out of you."

"It's okay," I said. "I've played the role before."

I got back to the set after the walk and saw Glenn Ford behind the corral where the wranglers were keeping the horses. He, also with time to kill, was practicing his fast-draw. Not many people know it, but Glenn is one of the greatest fast-draw artists of all time, maybe better than anybody in the Old West was. He's been clocked at four-tenths of a second.

"How's it going?" I asked, dipping into my own store of brilliant openers.

He studied the gun in his hand. "I think I'm pulling a little to the right. Wish I had some real bullets."

"Glad you haven't," I said. "I like this kind of thing better when it's all an illusion. Even like what we're doing here—a thirty-million-dollar illusion."

He tucked the .45 back into its holster. "Which could go up in smoke."

"Don't even talk like that. If it does, we all go up in smoke. Especially me, working for a percentage of the gross in lieu of a living wage."

"I know," said Glenn. "Me too. I still don't know how Lance talked us into it. Of course, I believe in this picture, the same as you do. It's just that—well, I don't know if *The Godless* is going to revolutionize the western, like *High Noon* or *Shane*, or if it's going to end up, brown and stuffed, on the Thanksgiving table."

"Oh, ye of little faith," I said.

He grinned. "Well, I'll admit it's got everything. Best seller, big, historical, true, and, of course, sexy. *Really* an adult western. Which sometimes just means that the plot's at least twenty-one years old. But even if

12

it is, it's being done very, very well. Very expensively. But nobody's made a western for years now, so the question is, how will they receive it out there?"

"Who knows? Audiences are like juries. You can't predict 'em."

"Or what little unseen factor might offend them. Did you hear Peter Revelstoke's latest radio bit?"

"That bastard," I said.

"They tape it from his TV shot and you can get it on shortwave. Peter Revelstoke, muckraker. And if there isn't any muck to rake, he'll shovel some in."

"So what's he been saying?"

"That the moral-majority types are already objecting to the picture. Not only for what they hear is in it, but for who's producing it."

"Lance Haverford? On account of that trouble he got into?" I rolled my eyes. "Let him among you who hasn't served eleven months for statutory rape cast the first stone."

"Eleven, with ten suspended, and a big, fat fine. Anyway, these people *can* hurt the picture with their boycott, come box-office time. If box-office time ever comes. I hear the budget's way over."

"Sure it is," I said. "That's part of Lance's genius." I was thinking about the trouble he'd gotten into and the publicity it had generated. The kid was fifteen, looked almost thirty, and was a tramp. Her old lady had set the whole thing up with a lawsuit in mind. None of this could be proved, but the judge must have suspected it and thus suspended most of the sentence.

"Well, let's hope for the best," said Glenn. "I'd better go now and see if they're through with Raquel. I'm on in scene 126."

"*Breck a fiess,*" I said, giving him the old actor's good-luck wish that he should break a leg.

He grinned. "Yiddish from an Irishman. The lingua franca of the motion picture industry."

"I thought lingua franca was something else," I said.

"Don't be dirty," said Glenn. "The script's bad enough as it is."

I moseyed down to the set to watch a few takes. They were doing a medium shot of Raquel Welch, just walking. Raquel Welch, just walking, isn't anybody just walking, and is something to see, all in itself. Especially since Raquel, in her tight dress, wasn't wearing any underwear. She ripples when she walks that way. All over. It's really something to see.

There had to be a lot of takes, even for this scene of a few seconds, until Lance Haverford, seeing flaws nobody else could see, was completely satisfied.

Lance was hovering over Joel Totterelli, who was supposed to be the director. If I had been Joel I would have resented it, but Joel, as long as he was off the sauce, was one of those real, sweet, unflappable guys, and that was his style. He'd won Oscars with it, like nearly everybody else in the picture.

The set where they were shooting now was one of several in the immediate area. In this broad valley, with those sawtooth hills in the background, a whole western town had been built, like the one John Wayne put up near Durango years ago. Most of it was facade—propped-up fronts rather than whole buildings—but Lance had insisted on authentic details down to the doorknobs which would never show on camera.

There's a probably apocryphal story about Eric von Stroheim insisting that the guardsmen extras in a period drama wear authentic underwear beneath their costumes. If I heard it about Lance Haverford, I'd half believe it. But, for all this, his stuff came out really first class, and a lot of people ranked him with Francis Ford Coppola.

I have watched him climb the crane with the director of photography, while the camera operator and the focus puller stood by, and, in animated discussion, tell them, more or less, how to do *their* jobs. I could see by their frowns that they didn't like it much, but Lance somehow made them swallow it. Up there on the crane, Lance, with his spade beard, plunging eyebrows, and burning eyes, looked more than ever like Satan. On a cliff, surveying the world.

Around the set, well off on the fringes, were the usual idle observers who always came from God knew where. Most were friends or acquaintances of somebody who had something to do with the picture. Most were from the town where virtually the entire company was staying in the one livable hotel there, drinking bottled water from the Canada Dry plant. If they drank water. Mescal, mixed with lemon soda—abominable stuff—was the in-drink and the usual choice of weapons in any drinking bouts that got started. John Wayne once drank a *Newsweek* reporter, who was following him around, under the table with mescal, leaving him there to be mopped up in the morning, and getting a very unfavorable story out of it; hijinks like that are rarer these days. Maybe all those millions they have to spend now has something to do with it.

All the people, and all it took to sustain them, and to make the picture, had been flown or trucked in long ago, in a logistical exercise Patton would have been proud of. The craft services included transportation, electrical, camera, sound, property, gaffers and grips—general handymen, so to speak—the wranglers with their horses, and the caterer. They came under the production manager, and he was under Phyllis Upton, the executive producer.

On the peculiar Hollywood totem pole, the executive producer is often not as high as the just-plain producer. But it's he or she who handles the nuts and bolts, frequently running everything when the producer is absent, tending to other projects. Phyllis was an absolute efficiency machine, well-respected, her astonishing competency much admired, even if she didn't get artistic hot flashes the way Lance did all the time.

I wondered what Phyllis thought about Lance taking most of the day for this short silent-action sequence that might even be edited out later. She oversaw the budget and the daily report of expenditures that was sent back to L.A. and she must have winced at the way the money was steadily shrinking.

I turned to Jennifer Schwartz, one of the production assistants. Her main job was to stand around with a clipboard tight against one swelling bazoom and look worried for Lance.

"Where's Phyl?" I asked.

"In the office trailer, sweating over the books, I guess," said Jennifer.

"With good reason," I said, nodding toward the preparations on the set for still another take.

"Yes. Over and over again on a little scene like this at God knows how many hundreds of dollars a minute. What's Lance trying to do—make Raquel feel special or something? As far as I'm concerned she's just another piece of decoration on the set—"

"A little more than that," I said mildly, so we wouldn't get into a big debate over it.

A male production assistant up near the camera apparently heard us talking and called out, "Quiet, please! Quiet, everybody!"

"Quiet?" I whispered to Jennifer. "There's no sound on this take."

She shrugged. "The way Mr. Haverford wants it."

Another assistant walked forward to smack the clapboards together. They give a sound-track cue but they were being used on this silent shot anyway. Abruptly, Lance Haverford held up his hand to stop everything. "Cut! Where the hell's Trish Wainwright?"

I looked at Jennifer. "No dialogue, but he wants the script girl. Where is Trish, by the way?"

"I don't know," said Jennifer. "Her highness is probably suffering from what women get at regular intervals. Or hope they do if they're in and out of as many beds as Trish Wainwright."

"Jennifer," I said, "remind me to send you a box of Meeow Mix sometime."

* * *

It now looked as though they'd be at least the rest of the morning on Raquel, so, after watching awhile, I decided to stroll again. I was tempted to cadge a ride back to the hotel and phone home just to see how Joan and Grandma and the kids were doing and learn whether the living room was still Grand Central Station with half the teen-age population of southern California passing through it. A touch of ennui kept me walking instead.

The top of a rise that overlooked the set seemed inviting. I climbed it, puffing a little. The high-protein diet is hard to stick to on caterer's fare. I made it to the crest finally, and stood there, scanning three hundred and sixty degrees, seeing everything, the whole panorama, the whole schmeer.

Far past the set, but still in the valley, was the old, ruined monastery: a sprawling, crumbled edifice, sad and beautiful in a bleeding-heart-of-Jesus sort of way—the climax scenes had already been shot there. Below me was the set itself: an authentic 1870s western town built with everything from a livery stable to a whorehouse, to say nothing of the antique steam engine that had been brought all the way here, along with tracks to run it on, for scenes that could much more easily have been shot back in L.A.—but that was Lance for you.

Next came all the trailers and a scattering of tent shelters, one of which was a small dispensary presided over by a Mexican doctor hired away from his patients in the town, who undoubtedly needed him more than we did.

I turned the other way and could see the city of Chirapulco a few miles off. Its one prominent modern building was the hotel, rising from a nexus of lovely older structures that had probably been there since the time of Coronado. Near the town was the airport, with our leased Cessna Citation SP II, looking like a toy in the distance, beside one of the hangars. The daily commercial plane didn't have direct connections with Los Angeles, so the jet was for flying in the dailies to the lab for processing, then back again, so we could all see what we'd been doing as we went along.

My own Cessna 182 was in one of the hangars. There were often two- or three-day stretches when I could get off, fly back and see the family. Something like the 182 would have done just as well for the dailies, but no, Lance had to have the Citation at about ten times the expense.

As I turned back toward the set now, I saw one of the local general handymen the key grip had hired running like hell toward it from the rolling, juniper-dotted hills and arroyos a little to the south—the area where I'd been strolling earlier that morning. He was stumbling and waving his arms and yelling something, though at this distance I couldn't make out what it was.

I trotted back toward the set. I reached it shortly after the handyman did, but as I approached I could see that there was considerable confusion over whatever it was he had said.

Jennifer Schwartz had backed away from everything, and she was standing, clipboard tight against her very major pectoralis, eyes wide and staring.

"Hey, Jenny," I called. "What's up?"

"Trish!" she said.

"What about Trish?"

"Out there in the arroyo—dead!"

"Dead?" I could feel myself get pale and frozen.

"Murdered!" she said, choking over it. "All carved up with a knife, he said!"

I stood there, looking stupidly at her, while it all sank in.

CHAPTER TWO

There are these laws of the universe, like you can never find a cop when you need one. They work in Mexico, too. Afterward, Dean Martin cracked that the way to do it here was to hold out a bribe, but that was when the initial shock and horror had died down.

I got to Trish Wainwright's body in the arroyo shortly after twenty or thirty other people did. I elbowed my way forward and saw it rag-dolled there, on the glistening ochre sand. The doctor—a small butterball of a man with a guardsman mustache—was already bent over it; he blocked a lot of my view, but not so much that I couldn't see the sickening worst of it. She was completely blood-smeared, and there were little crisscross knife cuts all over her, like those you put on a roast ham.

Phyllis Upton fetched up alongside me. She, too, stared at the body, and I tried, as always, not to stare too obviously at her. I felt guilty, being so conscious of Phyl's physical appearance; first, because she couldn't help it, and, second, because it had nothing to do with her admirable efficiency as an executive producer.

All I can say about the way Phyllis looked is that if a male brindled gnu came upon her he'd start his mating dance. Let's try to be nice about it and call her facial features strong instead of just plain ugly. Let's forget her squat figure with its legs by Steinway. Above all, please, let's not keep looking at her, wondering how it could possibly be.

"Poor Trish!" she said. "What kind of person could have done a thing like that?"

Oddly, her voice was nice; mellow and cultured.

I said, "Don't we have to notify somebody? The authorities? Her family?"

"I'll take care of it," said Phyllis.

She was a natural taker-care-of; the kind of person who does all the irritating or boring little jobs nobody else wants and finally ends up in charge of everything.

"I wonder," she said, still grimacing as she looked at the body, "if this kills the shooting for the rest of the day. God bless Trish's soul and everything, but I just can't help thinking about that. We can't afford to lose any more time. . . ."

As Phyllis had feared, we were through for the day. Lance called a halt to everything and most of us went back to the hotel to hang around. The truth—callous though it may sound—is that we'd have been better off working, making ourselves forget. But, of course, those of us who realized that couldn't very well say it. Probably our thoughts of the tragedy would have affected our performances. Anyway, a grinding halt—it couldn't be helped.

Mike Corby and I sat in the hotel cantina, drinking mescal and *limonada* and talking about this terrible state of affairs when Phyllis reappeared and descended upon us.

"Mike!" she said, looking harried. "You speak Spanish, don't you?"

He raised his battered countenance. "Some. It's of the Puerto Rican variety."

"Well, for God's sake," she said, "please come down to the police station with me. I can't seem to make them understand over the phone. What *is* the Spanish word for murder, anyway?"

"'*Asesinato,*'" said Mike. "Or '*homocidio.*' You learn it quick in Harlem."

After we hacked our way through a linguistic jungle at the police station—where, as a matter of fact, they already knew about the murder—the trail led us to the *capitano de descrubimientos,* or captain of detectives,

20

whose name was Alfonso Cruz. His home was a low, flat building near the center of town, with the usual fortified street front and the usual delightful, cactus-filled patio in the rear. Various women, who must have been his wife and other relatives, plus various young persons who must have been his children, showed us into the patio, and there was Cruz, twirling a cape and fighting a bull.

It wasn't a real bull; it was a set of horns on a wheelbarrow-like contraption, and a teen-age lad—one of his sons, no doubt—was charging him with this while he practiced *pasos naturales, rebolleras,* and all the rest.

There is a certain type of large, heavy man who has a peculiar grace and is light on his feet. Sidney Greenstreet, Laird Cregar, and Victor Buono, to all *requiescat in pace,* come to mind. Alfonso Cruz was like that. To my unpracticed eye what he was doing with that cape looked pretty good.

As it turned out, we didn't need Mike's Puerto Rican Spanish. Cruz folded the cape on his arm, turned to us, and said, in excellent English, "Good morning. You wish to talk to me about this terrible murder, no?"

"Oh," said Phyllis, pulled up short. "We thought you didn't know. Or the right people didn't know. Or somebody didn't care. Anyway, we do have to report it or something, don't we?"

Cruz smiled a little, obviously amused to see Phyllis slightly flustered. "The body, it is still in place?"

"Well, I don't know. Maybe the doctor took it to the dispensary. I couldn't just stay there and keep looking at it. It was so horrible. So—sadistic. It must have been bandits or something—"

"That is not likely, senora."

"Senorita," she corrected.

"Senorita." He nodded absentmindedly. "First, we no longer have bandits. Second, bandits would merely shoot her and not carve her with knives, as I understand has been done."

"Well, *somebody* did," said Phyllis.

"That is a valid assumption." Cruz delivered the line deadpan. "It is my guess that this is a crime of passion and that we may look to your own company to find out who committed it."

"Right," said Mike Corby. "One of those kinky jobs. Some kind of nut. I've seen it before."

Cruz leveled his ripe-olive eyes at Mike. "You have seen it before, senor?"

"I used to be a cop. New York Police Department."

"Of course!" said Cruz, recognizing Mike now, though I doubted that he was much of a movie fan. His smile teased the corners of his mouth. "And you are going to show us poor cousins south of the border how to do it, no?"

"Come off it, *capitano,*" said Mike. "The whole squeal's yours."

"Squeal?"

"Case. NYPD slang. They use different words on the West Coast—"

Cruz interrupted to jerk the conversation back into line. "We are not so poor and ignorant as you think, senor. You may be interested to know that I trained with the F.B.I. under the exchange program. Not that it helped my career a great deal. Here I am in the—what do you call them?—the boondoggles—"

"Boondocks," said Mike.

"*Sí*. And they have nothing but clowns in *El Capital,* where I thought I'd be assigned. The worst of it is that the *matadores* they send here are tenth rate and the bulls even worse. Well...one day, perhaps...when they take notice—"

"Maybe we better get out there, *capitano,*" said Mike.

"In a little time," said Cruz, nodding dreamily. "We do not rush into things down here, senor."

That evening, after Cruz and his team of detectives, which included a photographer, had done their stuff in the arroyo, and after the body had been removed to the hospital for an autopsy, Mike and I sat once more in the

22

cantina, where Jennifer Schwartz and Mariette Hartley joined us.

I liked having Mariette at the table. I could listen to that exquisite diction of hers all day. In *The Godless* she was perfect as the older sister who had returned from the East and hated the wild, wild West. Her performance, I was sure, would do even more for her career than those camera commercials she'd done with Jim Garner a few years before. An Oscar nomination maybe. If anybody ever got to see *The Godless*.

"What this guy Cruz ought to be doing," Mike said, "is looking into Trish Wainwright's background, finding out who she'd been associating with and things like that."

"Who *hadn't* she been associating with!" said Jennifer, her bazooms practically resting on the table as she leaned forward.

"Now, Jennifer," said Mariette, "the poor girl's dead."

Mike fastened his gunmetal eyes on Jennifer. "You seem to know a great deal about her."

"I know she slept around a lot. Not exactly in keeping with the airs she put on. She fancied herself a writer."

"Everybody does," I said, smiling. "It's a secret vice."

"She came out here against her family's wishes," Jennifer continued. "They're very big back East—stock market or something like that. You see them in mink and tuxes at all these big Guggenheim openings and things. But with all that bread behind her she had to be stubborn about it and make her own living. The way I hear it, she used her connections to get her job as script girl. Her connections and, uh, other assets. She was no stranger to the audition couch or any other kind of couch."

"Jennifer, you really shouldn't," said Mariette gently.

But Mike was interested. "Any idea who she was sleeping with around here?"

"You name it," said Jennifer, knowingly, mysteriously.

"It could be significant. With all that sadistic mutilation, this murder has sexual overtones, and maybe that's how it ought to be approached."

Mariette smiled. "Are you on the case already, Mike?"

"No, no," he said quickly. "Just thinking about it. You see, everybody has the wrong idea about how murders are solved. You seldom use a magnifying glass and make deductions, a la Sherlock Holmes."

"How is it done, then?" asked Mariette.

"Two ways, mainly," said Mike. "The first and most valuable aid to a working cop is a good stable of snitches. The second is files, which these days means computers. Tons and tons of stuff on record about all kinds of people, and you slog through it, sometimes for weeks or months, till you start to get patterns or connections. There's no glamor to it. Just dull, hard work."

"But the way you tracked down the Park Avenue Rapist wasn't exactly dull. Not in the book or the movie, anyway."

Mike shrugged. "Well, they hoked it up a little. The principle was the same. Cross-matching a lot of damn yellow sheets. It always boils down to as much background dope as you can get on the people involved."

Mariette sipped her drink daintily. It wasn't mescal; she didn't have to prove she was macho. "Mike, if you *were* trying to find out who killed poor Trish, just how would you start?"

"Out here? I don't know. I'd start talking to people who knew her well, I guess. Phone her family in New York. Routine R. and I. check with various agencies to see if she had a record. Poke around wherever she usually hung out."

"*El Pichon Azul*," said Jennifer. "The Blue Pigeon. The big cantina in town. Their version of the Cock and Bull. With that big local political boss whatsizname. And in his bed afterward, I've no doubt."

"It would be nice, Jennifer," Mariette said mildly, "if you *could* have a doubt once in a while."

"Anyway," said Mike. "That's what I'd do. Ask around."

"Are you going to?" asked Mariette.

"Naw. Alfonso Cruz would get his nuggets in an

24

uproar if I did. Of course, if he doesn't seem to get anywhere—"

I smiled at Mike. "What is it they say about old fire horses?"

"Forget it." Mike scowled. "I got enough on my mind without catching somebody else's squeal...."

The next day they got to my scene, which was with Genevieve Bujold. She was supposed to be the daughter of the French fire-engine inventor who had come to town, and she was giving me a bottle of imported wine, which I would spit out, wishing it were plain old red-eye. It was a cute scene, and I thought I played it funny, but Lance wasn't satisfied.

"George," he said, putting his hand on my shoulder and fixing me with that phony earnest look, "it's really Genevieve's scene, and I want it funny, but not so damned funny."

"Then favor Genevieve in the shot or put my dialogue O.S.," I said.

"George," he said, "let *me* do the directing."

I couldn't stop myself from saying, "I thought Joel was the director."

"He is, he is," Lance said quickly. "I'm just helping out a little here. Anyway, you know what I mean."

"Not yet," I said. "But I'll keep working on it."

Lunch, from the caterer's truck, was fried chicken. I found a makeshift table near the truck and Ira Yoder joined me. Ira loves fried chicken. Or anything else edible. He doesn't just eat; he wolfs. It was my guess he'd never had enough as a kid.

"They ought to be here any minute," said Ira.

"Who?"

"The media types. Ron Hendren, Rex Reed—even Mike Wallace."

"Mike Wallace? Kind of a big gun to be coming here, isn't he?"

"He was on his way to see the president of Mexico or somebody when he heard about the murder. Just curious, I guess, or maybe he's got some time to kill. I don't know. Anyway, they've all got clout, P.R.-wise. Including Peter Revelstoke, the schmuck. He's in the group, too."

Ira Yoder was small, excitable, sparrowlike. I always saw him as following horses to peck at their turds. He'd been engaged to do publicity for *The Godless*, and, like most of the others working on the project, he was a top man in his field. He was in and out on the set, usually with frantic ideas.

"A visitation from the media, huh?" I frowned. "Not too good. Everybody out in audienceland thinks we're a bunch of depraved alley cats to begin with, and a juicy murder won't do much to change that. God knows what Revelstoke will make of it."

"The only bad publicity," said Ira, trying to look wise and in control of everything, "is no publicity at all."

"Keep on saying that, Ira," I said, grinning at him, "and maybe one of these days you'll begin to believe it yourself."

With no camera call again, I was there to help greet the media luminaries when they arrived in a couple of sedans and a cloud of dust. Phyllis Upton had emerged from her trailer office to ramrod the affair, and she introduced everybody around as the reporters—celebrities in their own right—stepped from the cars.

Mike Wallace, whom I'd met before, said, "How you doin', George?"

"Pretty good," I said. "How's it going back in the center of the world?"

"Same old garbage and terror in the streets. It's still the place to be, though."

"That's what Mike Corby thinks," I said. "What in hell brings you here, anyway? The murder?"

"Not specifically. We've been thinking about an expose on shoddy bookkeeping practices in the motion-picture industry. You know, how stars agree to a percentage of the profits, and then there's never any profit showing. I just thought, since I was in the neighborhood, so to speak, I'd catch a little background atmosphere, maybe for future use. Peter Revelstoke's interested in your murder, though. He's been drooling all the way here."

By the time I caught up with Revelstoke, Ira Yoder had him in tow. As I approached, I heard Revelstoke, in that phony prep-school accent of his, saying, "But that's the way I wish to do it, Yoder. And I'll appreciate it if you arrange it for me properly, don't you know."

Revelstoke had high, thin nostrils and wore, with a tight tie, one of those short tab collars I thought had gone out with Franchot Tone or Robert Montgomery.

Ira, after we'd been introduced, summoned up his best distressed look and said to me, "Mr. Revelstoke wants to VTR his bit while Lance is actually shooting a scene in the background. Tell him, George. Tell him Lance will never go for it."

Revelstoke turned his eyes upon me and, from their royal blue depths, sent out a couple of laser beams. "So you're George Kennedy," he said. "One always recognizes you people, of course. It's one of the things wrong with Hollywood movies. One never enjoys the characters; one keeps seeing the same old stars. Who, frankly, for the most part, bore one."

"I heard you didn't like movies," I said, evenly enough.

"On the contrary," drawled Revelstoke. "I adore them. Good ones. Like *The Eternal Turnip*, which just won first prize at the Budapest festival. The symbolism was superb."

Not seeing much point in the debate he was inviting, I said, "What's this about taping your program on the set?"

"It should be obvious enough why I wish to do it that way. Verisimilitude. What I present, always, is the real truth that underlies the apparent truth. Who are these people, their shadows passing before us so magnified on the screen? What is their actual essence? It is, of course, one of sordidness and depravity, of utter falsehood and furious hype. This disgusting murder you've just had points it up nicely."

I stared at him. "Jesus! Are you for real?"

"I assure you I am," he said. "Tune in and find out."

Later, I watched him do his bit from the set, with his own videotape cameraman, whom he'd brought along. As I'd known, both Lance and Joel refused to shoot, or pretend to, while he was performing, even though Ira Yoder made an up-the-hill effort to persuade them. Revelstoke settled for speaking in front of a dead set, ad-libbing without cue cards; the guy was a skilled performer. That much had to be said for him.

I'd often wondered how Revelstoke's weekly broadcasts of industry gossip and critical reviews—always critical, mind you—got the ratings they did. For the same reason the *National Enquirer* sells a lot of papers, I imagine. Dirty underwear with the initials of someone famous upon it. He probably thought that if he ever said something good about anybody in the industry his rating would drop a couple of points. He may have been right, at that.

"Good evening one and all," said Revelstoke, giving his salutation the special, somehow haughty inflection that was his trademark. "I am speaking to you from the set of *The Godless* in Chirapulco, Mexico, where the makers of dreams are putting together another meretricious illusion to tarnish all our souls."

I looked at Ira, and Ira looked at me. Ira's look was that of a kid who has just discovered that there is no Santa Claus, or maybe that his mother and father had had to do *that* in order to have *him*.

"There has been a murder on this set," Revelstoke continued. "I am not surprised. Carelessness in moral behavior and utter contempt for what is true and beautiful can very well lead, in a series of insidious, unnoticed steps, to the ultimate transgression—the taking of life."

I whispered to Ira, "Does anybody really dig that?"

"How the fuck do I know?" Ira was almost crying.

"But that," continued Revelstoke, "is not what is

really significant, and, if I may say so, deliciously ironic about this murder. Regard, please. An attractive and innocent young woman—from a prominent family known for their good works and charities—has been cut off in the prime of life because, herself a victim of illusion, she dared to enter the sinkhole of atrocious taste that is known, generically, as Hollywood."

He rolled the "L's" in Hollywood as though he were performing oral sex upon the word.

"She met her epiphany," he said. "She was murdered. Horribly and brutally."

(I knew that this line in the broadcast would be accompanied by a still shot of Trish's blood-smeared body, which he could get for a few pesos from Cruz's people. He was a fine one to talk about good taste.)

"Murdered by person or persons unknown," he said. "And, I might add, under the very nose of a member of the cast—one who has been touted as a great detective! I am speaking, ladies and gentlemen, of Michael Corby, formerly a lieutenant of the New York Police Department, and now, to the despair of us all, an actor!"

It's not easy to make the word, "actor," sound like pimp, traitor, or habitual perpetrator of barratry on the high seas, but Revelstoke managed.

"It is significant," he said. "Archetypical. The abilities of policemen, like all else in Hollywood, are illusion—a blown-up shadow!"

There was more. A little over three minutes' worth, altogether—enough time for his verbal talons to leave a number of discernible gashes. Ira and I took it all in and afterward felt as though we'd just been forced to witness a flogging.

That evening, in the hotel cantina, Lance and Ira and I discussed it over drinks. I risked having to turn in my badge by having the more palatable tequila in my *limonada* instead of mescal. Ira had the canned cream soda he'd brought with him.

"So Revelstoke put us through the wringer again," he said. "But at least he mentioned the picture and got

29

a bunch of names in. Maybe it's not *too* bad. Maybe, in fact, all this crap about moral depravity will just make 'em want to come and see the picture more."

"That's your department," said Lance. "I wouldn't try to outguess public reaction. If I could, I'd be in the stock market or something instead of getting ulcers as a producer."

"You got ulcers, Lance?" asked Ira.

"Not yet, but don't go 'way," Lance said. "Anyhow, it's not so much *public* reaction that worries me."

"Yeah? What does?"

"J. Sutton Fargo."

"Oh. Him," said Ira.

"At the mention of his name you may all bow three times toward L.A. Unless he's gone back to Texas."

"What about J. Sutton Fargo?" I asked. "I know he's our principal backer, but what's it got to do with Revelstoke's broadcast?"

"You haven't met him yet, George," said Lance. "But you will. His dim-witted wife, anyway. She's the main reason he put so much of his own money, and that of his cronies, into the picture—so she could rub elbows with all the stars. Five million smackeroonies, right out of the salt domes of Texas, where he stole it in the first place. He's got more oil than a goddamned Arab. Without his five mil', we never would have gotten the rest from the banks. And if we run over budget—which we will—the overflow's got to come from J. Sutton Fargo."

"You can always get another million or two after spending thirty, can't you?" I asked, feeling a little heady talking about millions as though they were loose change one carried in one's pocket.

"Not always," said Lance. "Take MGM. Big outfit—everybody knows them. But broke, deep in debt. They wanted to fix up Natalie Wood's almost-finished picture when she drowned—it was sure box office—and they just didn't have what we may refer to as another lousy million. So if we need some post-production funds Fargo's our only possible source."

"What makes you think he might not spring?"

"Little things like a murder might put him out of the mood. He's a big follower of the Crusade for Decency movement, or whatever the hell they call it. Goes to tent revivals like we might go to basketball games. I wouldn't put it past him, if he gets upset, to write off his whole goddamned five million and drop the project. He'd probably get some kind of favorable tax loss out of it, anyway."

I frowned at my tequila. "Would it help if Mike *could* find out who murdered Trish, and why? You know—as though we cleaned up our own backyard."

"I don't know," said Lance. "I just know we can't afford any more trouble in the morals department."

"There won't be any," said Ira.

"Don't say that," snapped Lance. "I'm superstitious. . . ."

CHAPTER THREE

The location for the cliff sequence wasn't far from the western town. If Lance had been following his usual practice as a certified genius he'd have gone to Morocco or Hong Kong or some damn place for just the right cliff. But here it was, a burro ride from Chirapulco.

Revelstoke and the few other media types who were still on hand were invited to watch the filming of the spectacular leap from the cliff—an episode written in, by the way, after the location scouts had spotted the precipice. Ira felt that such a diversion might take their minds off the murder or any other peccadilloes they had in mind.

I decided to watch, too, and hopped into the jeep beside Wally Demarest, the stunt man. In size and build Wally resembled the actor he was stunting for. He was big, blond, lean, and well-muscled. All the time he'd evidently spent on the development of his body hadn't left much for his mind. He seldom said anything you had to think too hard about, and in that respect, it was refreshing to be with him if you happened to need a breather.

The jeep jolted over the donkey trail, a grip driving, Wally and me in the back seat. "How's the stunt today?" I asked. "Any problems?"

"Piece o' cake, George," he said. "I ran through it real good yesterday. I mean, not everybody could hit that air mattress ninety feet down, but I got it worked out now. You know I dove down at Acapulco a coupla times? On network TV."

"No, I didn't. Must be a real thrill."

"Yeah, it was okay. The prize money was peanuts, though. Shit, what I get for doing this is peanuts."

"Come on, Wally," I said. "Lance always pays you over scale. You must be doing okay."

"For stunt pay, maybe. What I mean is, stunt pay is peanuts. Not like actors get. We put our asses on the line and they get all the bucks, all the glory."

"Well, that's the way it is. Actors are who the public pays to see. How hard they work, compared to stunt men or anybody else, is beside the point. It's the law of supply and demand."

"Just the same," said Wally, in his high-pitched, breathy voice, "the actors got it made. They couldn't do my job in a million years. But I could do theirs, easy."

"Acting's not always as easy as it looks," I said.

"Shit!" he said, unwrapping a stick of sugarless gum and popping it into his mouth. "What's there to it? You memorize a few lines and step in front of the camera and say them. Sometimes you don't even have lines. You just walk, or sit there and scratch your ass or something."

There was no time to explain to Wally all the things that go into a good, professional acting performance, and besides, I wasn't sure he'd understand a lot of them. And I certainly didn't want to upset him by telling him that scratchy voice of his would keep him from ever being an actor—at least one with any romantic appeal. By his very manner of speech and the look in his eye, he'd be limited to playing dumb guys, which he was. And I don't say that pejoratively. Some of my best friends are dumb guys.

"Well," I said, "it's like anything else. You have to practice first."

"And get the breaks."

"That, too," I admitted.

"You'd think Joel or somebody would let me try," said Wally, unwilling to let go of what I now began to suspect was his favorite obsession. "Just a walk-on part, or something. To get started. Look, I don't want to sound conceited or something, but I ain't exactly grotesque, right? I could get all the broads I wanted—if I wanted broads—so why in hell wouldn't they want to look at me in the movies?"

"It's more than being good-looking," I said. "Whatever you project, whatever comes out from inside, is elusive—very hard to explain."

"Yeah, I've heard that before, and it's bullshit," he said. "They'd like to have your bod' or they wouldn't. That's what it boils down to. Know what they called me when I was rassling a few years back? Kid Apollo. You shoulda heard the broads in the audience moan and scream when I came on."

"Well, it's an asset," I said. "But it still isn't the whole bag."

"Look at Sly Stallone and Schwarzenegger. I got a bod' as good as them. Better. They're overmuscled."

"Uh-huh," I said, seeing no need to argue.

"You know why I never get a real break in this business? It's on account of my—you know—my sexual preferences!"

I shook my head, a little surprised to find Wally so candid with me. Not that he ever tried to cover up his homosexuality, but he never made it a topic of conversation, either. And he didn't lisp or mince or swish or make a limp wrist, or do any of those other things that gays are supposed to do, so if you didn't know Wally Demarest you'd never guess he was anything but macho in his spare time. Besides, he was a stunt man, and that's strictly a male society; that made Wally an extremely rare exception. And so, because his sexual orientation just plain didn't show, I couldn't believe—as he apparently did—that it had interfered with his career. "Hang in there, Wally," I said. "You might get a break one of these days. You never know. And when you do, cheer up. Nobody ever lost a job in Hollywood because he was gay."

I didn't believe Wally ever would get a break, but that was about as much as I could say without plunging him into a state of despair, which I didn't think would be wise just before his stunt.

There was less of a crew and fewer observers at the stunt scene than we usually had back at the town set, but it was still a sizeable gathering. The cliff was part of a deep gorge cut through the high desert plateau; there was a trickling stream at the bottom that became a river a little farther on. Joel had called for four cameras on this scene so that there would be several angles for editing; because of both the danger and expense the action could be done only once, with no retakes.

Ira Yoder was mother-henning our guests from the media, keeping them out of the way and busily explaining things he really didn't know too much about. That was okay; they didn't know too much about them, either, so they drank it all in.

Looking for a place to sit and watch I spotted Sam Rubicoff, the stunt coordinator, sitting on a rock, shelling peanuts from a paper sack, and eating them one by one. Sam was a barrel-chested man with muscular, hairy fore-arms, a pair of fierce dark eyes, and a scowl an old pirate of the Spanish main would have been proud of. Sam and I went way back to the early days of TV, when series like "Gunsmoke" and "Have Gun Will Travel" were being shot on location in such places as Eugene, Oregon, around the Three Sisters Mountains. In nine working days we'd shoot about three half-hour shows, which today probably seems incredible.

"Sit down, George." Sam patted the rock beside him. "Have a peanut. I know you're not in this scene, so what are you doing here?"

"Killing time. As usual. Why should we kill time, I wonder? It's too important to be dead."

"If you're going to discuss philosophy," said Sam dryly, "go find yourself a philosopher someplace. Me, I'm just a glorified stunt man. Too creaky in the joints to do it myself any more, so I coordinate other guys. What the hell. It's a living."

35

"At least you don't think you're an undiscovered actor."

"Like Wally?" He laughed. "Don't be too sure about that. I used to get bit parts back in the old 'Gunsmoke' days in addition to the stunts I was doing. You know what? I don't think I was too bad."

"Take my word for it, Sam. You were better risking your ass in long shots. The longer the better. Like Wally's doing today." I nodded toward the cliff edge, where camera assistants were checking the lighting from the shiny-boards on Wally as he measured the steps of his running approach and gauged his falling distance.

Sam contemplated Wally for a moment. "Yeah, there's always that element of risk, even when you set it up as carefully as you can. Which I tried to do with Wally, by the way, so he wouldn't just go into it without any preparation. I made him take that practice fall yesterday so he'd know exactly how to hit the air bag. The timing's very critical. He's got to take the precise number of running steps at just the right speed or he'll be off target. But he's basically a good athlete; he knows what he's doing."

"I hope so," I said. "That goddamned air bag looks awfully small from ninety feet up. I get dizzy just looking down at it."

"So don't look," grinned Sam. He held out the paper sack. "Have another peanut."

The cameras were ready now and Joel Totterelli was off to one side, waiting for the right moment to call for action. Wally Demarest was perhaps twenty paces back from the edge of the cliff, with a production assistant beside him, and this assistant was pouring his usual Gator Ade into a paper cup for him.

I frowned and glanced at Sam. "That wouldn't be booze Wally's taking just before a stunt, would it?"

Sam shook his head. "Not Wally. He's a health nut. He's got more theories about what's good or bad for you than Johns Hopkins. One of 'em is that the Gator Ade gives you quick energy and sharpens your sense of timing. I don't know if it does or not, but Wally believes it and that's what counts."

I must mention the production assistant who handed Wally his Gator Ade. If I do not mention him he will disappear like those little men in black who come on stage in Japanese Kabuki plays to change the set while the action continues. Like almost all male production assistants, this one was young, nice-looking, well-educated, and basically dumb. He gave Wally his drink and dissolved himself back into the air again.

Wally was ready to go, but there was now another brief delay as Joel apparently decided to recheck everything. The scene absolutely had to go right the first time; if it didn't they'd have to reshoot again at thousands of dollars an hour, and we were behind schedule and over budget already.

At last the moment of truth could be put off no longer. Joel, clean-shaven and in neat khakis with an L.L. Bean look, nodded and said something quiet...another production assistant smacked the clap-boards together. Joel cued Wally by pointing his finger.

Wally started his run forward. His timing and his careful placement of his steps resembled the choreography of a champion pole vaulter as he went into his approach. For a fleeting moment it struck me, in a dim, subconscious way, that *something* was wrong. ESP? I don't know—I get these odd stirrings and premonitions sometimes. I can't prove it; you'll have to take my word for it.

Wally reached the edge of the cliff and went flying into the air. Somehow, not as gracefully as I'd thought he would—he seemed to falter just before the leap. I figured, in the next second or two, that I was just seeing it wrong.

The bottom of the gorge was rocky, a quarter-mile floor around the stream that could be a torrent when it rained. A spot where it was relatively flat at the base of the cliff had been chosen for the stunt. It wasn't all that flat. There were still sharp rocks all around the inflated,

37

twenty-foot-square, heavy-plastic air bag. From where we sat, on an inward curve of the gorge, Mike and I could see the mattress below, along with the men who stood near it but out of camera range. With everyone well aware of the stunt's potential danger, they kept stretchers and first-aid supplies ready.

We saw Wally hit, flat on his back. Not on the mattress, but just beside it. I gave a sickened gasp and rose and ran forward.

That was what just about everybody did....

At the bar of the hotel cantina that evening, Mike Corby and I each ordered a cold bottle of Dos Equis. Good beer, but we hardly tasted it. It gave us something to do with our hands.

"Every time I think of it," I said, still half in a state of shock—

"Yeah." Mike nodded.

The cantina was crowded with members of the company and our visitors from the media. There was a buzzing of talk in the air, but there was little merriment in it.

"The doc did his best in that dispensary tent," I said. "Wally was still alive when they got him there. Just barely. I don't think anybody could have saved him."

"Yeah," said Mike again.

"He was so confident," I said. "He told me the stunt would be a piece of cake."

"Maybe it was," said Mike. "All things being equal. Which I don't think they were."

"What do you mean?"

Before Mike could answer, Peter Revelstoke strolled up and invited himself onto a stool beside us. For the evening, he had donned what looked like an Abercrombie and Fitch bush jacket with a paisley cravat on his neck. Muttering, he ordered a sweet vermouth on the rocks from the bartender, and the bartender, with a faint look of disapproval, went off to fetch it. Then he turned and regarded us for a moment with his royal blue eyes as though we were having an environmental impact upon the surroundings.

"Detestable, isn't it?" he said. "A man dies to provide a cheap thrill for the mass worshipers in the temples of tacky entertainment."

"Get lost, Revelstoke," I said.

He merely smiled a little and kept his eyes on us. "The illusion of someone falling from a cliff could have been created just as well without the actual danger, don't you know. With a dummy, perhaps, or, better yet, by suggestion or symbolism. But no. The director has to show the actual fall, mistaking naive realism for artistic excellence. And now you have more than the tragedy of this young man's untimely demise. You have troubles that may well accumulate and destroy your entire effort. It's hardly worth preserving, of course, but I find it quite sad that it takes the loss of two lives to bring about that result."

"I've had it with you, Revelstoke," I said, trying to keep it in a normal tone of voice, which wasn't easy.

"I didn't expect you to understand," he said. "But you should, with some guidance, be able to grasp the plain facts. The rumor has already been kindled. *The Godless* is jinxed. The public loves such superstition. And they are not alone in this. Actors are particularly prone to irrational beliefs. I've heard several dark surmises this evening—no one's saying it in so many words, but the undercurrent of meaning is there. I wouldn't be the least bit surprised to see one or two of your stars walk off the set in superstitious fear."

"Listen," I said, "if there are any rumors like that, you probably planted them. For the sake of something juicy to put in your broadcast."

He shook his head. "You think it's personal. It's not. I've nothing against you or anyone else in the company in a personal sense. My only concern is with artistic taste; my function in society is to improve its standards, don't you know. But many people out there will consider the moral aspect alone. They will see these deaths as just punishment for sins committed. That is nonsense, of course, but it exists, and must be dealt with."

"What can I do to make you go away?" I said. "Close my eyes?"

By this time the bartender had brought Revelstoke's drink and set it before him. Revelstoke took the drink and laid money on the bar. "Very well," he said. "I'll find someone more responsive. It's futile to discuss anything requiring a measure of thought with Hollywood types. Good evening, gentlemen."

"Hey, Revelstoke," Mike said quietly.

"Yes?"

"Up yours, huh?"

Revelstoke stalked off.

Mike and I looked at each other. I said, "Ira won't be happy with us. He wants us to be nice to the media."

"Being nice to that guy wouldn't help," said Mike. "Let's just hope he doesn't start guessing too much about what happened to Wally. What maybe happened, anyway."

"You were hinting at something when Revelstoke walked up. What was it, Mike?"

He frowned thoughtfully. "You saw him run and jump. His timing was all off. I saw his practice run yesterday and it was a lot different. He wasn't half-stumbling; he was sure of what he was doing."

"What are you trying to say, Mike?"

"His concentration was off. Why? Well, all I've got is a wild guess, and it could be wrong. That Gator Ade he drank. What if—just try this for size now—what if something in the Gator Ade affected his reflexes, threw him all off?"

"That *is* wild. How could it be?"

"I don't know, exactly. But if there was something in the stuff it could have had time to work while Joel was setting up the shot. So...while everybody was crowding around poor Wally, where he'd fallen, I picked up the bottle and what was left in it."

"Don't tell me you found something!"

Mike shook his head. "I smelled it and tasted some from my finger, but there didn't seem to be anything wrong. It would probably have to be analyzed in a lab. I've got friends with LAPD who'd do it, if I asked."

"So what are you going to do, send it to them?"

"I've been debating that. Like you say, it's wild, and the odds are I'm wrong. On the other hand, in all the years I've been a cop I've seen the damndest things happen, and sometimes I've latched on to them through no more than a goofball hunch like the one that's hitting me now. What I'm really saying, I think, is that you shouldn't ignore any detail, even if it seems farfetched."

I nodded, digesting what he'd said. "Look," I said finally, "I'll tell you what. I won't be on call for a couple of days and I thought I'd fly back in the Cessna to see the family and take care of a few other things. I could give you a lift and you could get that thing analyzed, if you want. That way, even if it turns out to be nothing, you won't be wondering about it."

"Okay," he said. "I'd rather fly with you than ride in the jet when it takes the dailies in."

"The Citation's a lot faster. And perfectly safe."

"It's not the airplane—it's the company."

"Ferdy? He's okay."

"The hell he is," said Mike. "He's a leaping, screaming Nazi."

"He isn't old enough to be a Nazi."

"Well, he's the next thing to it."

"He hasn't struck me one way or the other," I said. "All Ferdy Holtz and I ever talk about is flying. Anyway, if you want a ride we'll take off in the morning."

"Yeah," said Mike, draining his beer. "Better than hanging around here and just waiting all the time."

CHAPTER FOUR

I sat with J. Sutton Fargo at an umbrella-covered table beside the swimming pool in the luxury hotel where he had two adjoining pool-side suites. A Filipino in a white coat brought the vitamin-laced fruit drink he'd had the hotel concoct from his own recipe. To me it tasted like Hawaiian Punch, right out of the can, but Fargo was full of praise for what he firmly believed to be both its deliciousness and its magical powers as far as one's health was concerned.

I think everybody has little crotchets like this. It's just that when they get very, very rich they can indulge them.

I had promised Lance Haverford I'd call on Fargo when I got to L.A., for several oddball reasons, though Lance was quite serious about them. First, Lance had said, he knew I was a family man (it could have been a left-handed compliment and it could have meant Lance thought I was a square, which in many ways I guess I am), and he wanted Fargo to see that some of our cast members were just plain folks, not given to the nightly orgies so many outsiders believe to be the norm in Hollywood. Second, he wanted me to assure Fargo that everything was going just fine on location, in spite of what he might have heard about one murder and one accidental death, and that the five million he'd put into the enterprise—some of it from his cronies, but all of it under his control—was still safe. Third, he wanted me to pave the way for a request for additional funds to take care of the overrun that was just about certain now. You know, that lousy one or two million; and I still get a feeling of committing blasphemy when I say it that way.

Finally, Lance knew that Fargo's wife, Marilou, wanted to meet me, just as she wanted to meet anybody who appeared with even modest frequency on what I'll bet she referred to as the silver screen. Making her happy was the same as keeping Fargo on the hook.

"Marilou'll be here in a minute, George," said Fargo, showing a half-smile that said, We men understand about women, don't we? "She wanted to put on somethin' nice to meet you."

"She didn't have to," I said, "but if it makes her feel good, that's fine."

"The gals," said Fargo. "Can't live with 'em, and can't live without 'em."

I had an idea all his aphorisms, like that one, were ready-made.

I'm as prone to stereotyping as the next guy, and if you had asked me to describe a typical wealthy Texan I'd have said somebody big and overbearing, coming on strong, and wearing a ten-gallon hat. Fargo had the hat somewhere, I supposed, but the rest of that didn't at all fit him. He was a small, neat man who spoke rather softly and wore a well-tailored tropical suit that looked more Brooks Brothers than it did Nieman Marcus. His accent was mellow rather than strident, and it added to the air of old-fashioned courtesy that surrounded him. But he wasn't altogether a soft man. His eyes, which could get hard and chilly once in a while, showed that.

"You sit right where you are, George," he said, rising, "and I'm gonna show you somethin'."

He disappeared through the door of the suite and I waited and sipped my fruit drink. It was an unusually gray day—not smog but genuine fog—and no one was using the pool, so I didn't even have any stacked figures in bikinis to look at. I hoped Fargo wouldn't keep me too long, because Mike Corby had promised to call me at home around lunchtime with, he hoped, the results of the lab tests on the Gator Ade. I've often wondered about

Gator Ade. Do some people believe it has boiled alligators in it instead of all those citrus fruits that are supposed to keep you going in the most grueling of athletic contests?

Fargo was back in a moment with a gunbelt and holster in his hands. He placed it on the table. The leather, old and dry, seemed about to crumble in places. "Pick it up but be careful," he said. "Any idea whose it was?"

"Your great grandfather's? Something like that?"

"Earp's," he said.

For a moment I thought it was his stomach.

"Wyatt Earp's," he continued. "I had it all checked out carefully, and it really did belong to the famed lawman himself. Paid a pretty penny for it to another collector here in southern California. George, you're holding history in your hands."

"I'm impressed." I was. "I didn't know you were a collector." Of anything but money, was what I meant.

"In a modest way," said Fargo. "Might open up a museum one o' these days. You see, there's more to it than just historical interest. The Old West represents the true moral fiber of our country, which is goin' right out the window today. Sexual permissiveness, narcotics, the coddling of criminals. Unless we want to fall, like the Roman Empire, we've just got to go back to those old ways."

"There's something to what you say," I admitted, "but it's a complicated question."

"Nothin' complicated about it. Show folks what's right and they'll respond to it. Movies can be a powerful influence and that's why I put up a few million for that western of yours. If I can also make a nickel profit, well, that's all to the good."

I looked a little puzzled. *The Godless,* I said, "is one hell of a western, but it's not exactly a play you'd put on in Sunday School."

"Exactly. These are modern times, George, and the Devil's got a good foothold. If you're gonna get people's attention, you gotta throw sex and that kind of thing in.

44

I'm not naive about that. But, basically, *The Godless* is still an old-fashioned morality play, with the good guys winning out in the end."

"I suppose it is."

"And what I'm doin' is boring from within. Using what influence I can on the script and the finished product. I know Lance Haverford resents my occasional suggestions, but he needs my money and can't afford to get too damned artistic about it and scream at me to keep my cotton-pickin' fingers off. What I can do—what I am doin'—is keepin' this movie from gettin' *too* damned dirty and depraved and makin' sure its basic message of old-fashioned morality doesn't get lost."

I smiled a little. "I'll say this much for you, Mr. Fargo—"

"Call me Sut."

"Sut. You lay your cards on the table."

"Damn right. Honesty's another old-fashioned virtue that pays in the long run. George, I'd like you on my side. I'd like you to do whatever you can, wherever you can, to see that this picture doesn't get out of hand."

"I'm not sure I have all that much influence," I said. There was no point in adding that the way I saw it, Lance was trying to make a reflection of history, not a thinly disguised sermon, and that I had no intention of interfering with this.

Before the discussion could get so tangled up I couldn't find my way out of it, Marilou Fargo appeared, and we both rose to greet her with a smile. She, too, was small, and also slightly plump. Her hair—almost certainly getting gray in its natural state—was rinsed to a sandy blonde and nicely done up. An almost daily visit while she was here to some hairdresser to the stars, I would bet. She had dressed herself in a sailor-suit thing— my wife would probably know the technical term for it. The total effect was not at all unattractive; there was even a subliminal touch of sex in it, though I'm not sure why.

"Joe-werdge Kennedy!" she said, beaming and taking my hand. That was how she pronounced my first name, in two distinct syllables. "Why, you look just like you do on the screen! I just love you in those *Airport* movies, where you play that Italian engineer, or whatever he is. The only thing I'd say is that you don't really look Italian."

"A lot of Italians don't," I said. "Same goes for any ethnic group. Including Texans."

Both Fargo and Marilou thought this much funnier than it was.

"In Texas," said Fargo, "we say you should never ask a man where he's from. If it's Texas, he'll tell you soon enough. If it's not, well, you don't want to make him feel bad."

I gave that one a little more laughter than it deserved.

Marilou sat, looked at the pitcher of fruit juice, and said, "Sutton, there must be somethin' better than this around."

"Kind of early," he said, with a frown.

"Well," said Marilou, "it's just not proper hospitality not to offer a guest—especially Joe-werdge here—a proper drink. Myself, I think I'll have a whiskey sour."

"Nothing for me," I said. "I have to leave in a few minutes, anyway."

"Oh. I was hopin' you could stay for lunch, Joe-werdge. Sutton has to go out again, and maybe we could enjoy a little swim. I'd like to take a few pictures with my little ol' Polaroid."

Fargo chuckled. "Then she shows 'em to all her gal friends back home and that's supposed to impress 'em. What really happens is, they get jealous."

"Now, Sutton," she said.

There was something in Marilou Fargo's look as she kept tossing it at me. A wicked little smile feathering the edge of her budded lips. I can't be sure of this, and I almost hate to say it, but I think the message was that if I hung around we might *really* get acquainted. I wasn't about to do that, not even for the sake of the picture. Let Lance Haverford go that route. He'd probably fool around for the sake of fooling around, picture or no picture. But to think that was getting gossipy, just like Jennifer Schwartz.

The rest of the conversation was all about what movie stars I knew personally—actually fairly few—and what were they really like—and then, after a few fidgety glances at my watch, I worked up to a point where I could politely excuse myself.

Marilou planted a wet kiss on my cheek as I left, and made me promise to come again sometime. J. Sutton Fargo told me he was glad to have me on his side—which I hadn't said I was—and both came out to the lobby with me, where I got stopped for a couple of autographs, and waved good-bye as I climbed into the Benz.

I supposed I'd left a good impression, as Lance had hoped I would, and, to that extent, it was mission accomplished. But I was faintly uncomfortable. I had the feeling that Fargo, precisely because he wasn't backing the picture as a cold business proposition, might still pull out of it one of these days for purely emotional reasons if something we did or failed to do rubbed his fur the wrong way.

By the time I got back to the tucked-away house on a winding drive in Encino, Madlyn, my secretary, a slim brunette with a great phone voice, already had a notation that Mike Corby had called. The kids and their friends were streaming in and out all in a flap about a camping trip and a misplaced sleeping bag—for some reason they always wanted me to drop everything and solve such problems personally—but in spite of this I managed to make phone contact with Mike at his downtown hotel.

"George, listen to this!" Mike said excitedly. "They ran that Gator Ade through the test tubes and everything. You know what? It had enough barbiturates in it to put an elephant to sleep!"

"Jesus!" I said.

"Yeah," said Mike. "That's about what *I* said."

CHAPTER FIVE

For Mike, getting into the investigation, as he did, was a little like a man getting bald. There was no one moment, nor even one day, when a perceptible change came along. At first, as he'd told Mariette Hartley, he was a mildly interested observer, off to one side. Now, suddenly, he was poking into the matter.

But with the lowest of profiles. In fact, for a day or two after we returned from Los Angeles, I was the only one in the location area who knew Mike was investigating. And even I didn't know exactly how he was going about it.

All I knew was what Mike had told me on the airplane during the return trip, which required the usual stops at airports of departure and entry and the usual hassle with the officials we encountered. Ordinarily, the Mexican authorities are masters of bureaucratic delay, and what's behind all their fussing and maneuvering is the desire of the Mexican government to have visitors use their official airlines instead of private planes. They have a rule that an aircraft that goes out must have aboard exactly the same personnel when it comes in again, but Lance, the miracle worker, had managed to modify this for members of the company. He probably made a huge political contribution, but, anyway, we flew in and out with relative ease and with some of the usual rules waived.

With good weather and clear skies, there had been lots of time for talk as Mike sat beside me, and I let him handle the controls once in a while, just for fun.

"Don't worry about a thing, Mike," I said, grinning. "Sylvester the cat will keep her up."

Sylvester, the mangy, bewhiskered cartoon character, is painted on my airplane, where he holds a red balloon. He hangs in the cockpit and on the dashboard of my car. I don't know why. If anybody asks me why I say, Why not?

"Then let him fly the damned thing," said Mike, letting go of the yoke. I could almost hear him shift gears in his head. "They got a pretty good crime lab at LAPD," he said. "And a lot of expertise available in all the universities nearby. They can handle some pretty sophisticated stuff. Analyzing the Gator Ade was no problem."

"Barbiturates, you said."

"Specifically, sodium secobarbital, which you can get in any high school locker room. Comes in capsules known variously as redbirds or red devils. One of the so-called 'downers.' A hundred milligrams'll make you, like, drunk. A few hundred can kill you. The effect can last for hours and takes hold in a few minutes. It was enough to throw Wally Demarest way off, so he missed the air mattress. The murderer probably wasn't depending on his missing that mattress."

"Why in his Gator Ade? Why not in his coffee or something?"

"One, because only Wally drank it, and two, because all that citrus masks any taste. Actually, at this point we don't know for sure that anybody did it to him. Maybe *he* broke a capsule and emptied it into his Gator Ade. Or maybe it just got in accidentally. We can't say with absolute certainty that it was a murder."

"Well, if it wasn't," I answered, "it was a hell of a coincidence, coming right on top of Trish Wainwright's murder."

"Sure. Only it's the kind of coincidence that can throw you off. All the two deaths have in common is that they were close in time to each other. If both were murder, they could still be separate. Each had a different M.O. A guy who stabs is different, psychologically, from

49

a guy who poisons. If anything, what we have here points to two different persons."

"I guess you're right," I said. "Though I still have this funny feeling that somebody's out to sink the picture and is taking all this trouble to do it. Or is that too far-out?"

"It's a possibility," said Mike. "But, right now, anything's a possibility. What I'm telling you about the M.O. is what is *likely*. Exceptions do come along, of course. A clever killer, for example, could use more than one *modus operandi* just to divert suspicion. That's happened before, but it's pretty rare. Right now, all this is empty speculation. First step is to find out all we can about the victims, and then see if there are any patterns."

"Which you're going to do?"

"Oh, I don't know. I guess I'll look into it a little more. Something to do, with all this time on my hands, waiting for camera calls. But keep it under your hat, okay, George?"

I didn't exactly forget about Mike's findings in the next couple of days, but I did manage to stick the whole affair on a mental shelf for a while. With several camera calls to meet—all the reporters had gone and we were shooting steadily now—I didn't see much of Mike and focused my attention on the picture.

Because I'd agreed to a profit-participation deal, I had more than a hired hand's interest in the success of the enterprise. That was why I took the time to give Blossom Foster a little help.

We sat in the living room of her suite in the hotel, with a script opened on the coffee table in front of us. She had a whole suite not because she was a star—not yet, at any rate—but because her mother was with her and there had to be room for both of them.

Blossom was nineteen, and, in appearance, fresh as a pail of buttermilk. Even her long hair had that pale, slightly creamy look of buttermilk. Ira Yoder, in his publicity releases, was calling her the buttermilk blonde.

He'd also invented a story that Lance Haverford had discovered her sipping a vanilla shake in a burger joint one day, but the truth was she'd originally shown up with a group of other hopefuls for a mass audition that was, in itself, primarily a publicity gimmick. The minute she'd walked in the room she'd set off vibes—the way Marilyn Monroe used to do. Every eye settled on her principal charms. All two of them.

With only some dramatic training in high school plays, Blossom needed work on her voice, on how she carried herself, and even on the way she dressed and used makeup. But underneath this unpolished exterior was an elusive quality Lance had spotted at once. There was something both womanly and childlike about her. You wanted to protect her and ravish her all at once.

Lance lost no time in giving her a screen test to find out if this quality registered on film. It did, and he gave her the feature part. Glossies of her in everything from blue jeans to pelvic shoestrings had already been distributed—to hang, I had no doubt, in a number of locker rooms and on fraternity-house walls; in the credits she would be billed full screen.

AND INTRODUCING—BLOSSOM FOSTER

Although all I had in mind was to give Blossom a little coaching, I must confess that sitting next to her there on the couch, feeling her warmth and vibrancy and getting brushed by her once in a while as she moved, stirred what red corpuscles I have left. Only a robot would have been immune to it.

"'But you don't know how lonely I've been,'" she said, reading a line from the script. She swung her large, apple-green eyes upon me. "Where do I put the accent, George? On 'you,' or 'know,' or on 'lonely'? I can't seem to get it right."

"Don't worry about which word to hit," I said. "All you do is concentrate on the meaning of the line. Say it the way you yourself would say it if you were actually in the situation. Come on, let's take it from the top again."

Before Blossom could give it another try, her mother, Cora, walked in, returning from some errand or other. "Well," she said, "I see you two are still at it."

In a way, she was a better actress than Blossom. She managed to get hidden meaning into her seemingly innocuous speech. The hidden meaning was that she believed she'd returned just in time to prevent us from indulging in hanky-panky there on the couch. She wouldn't have minded the hanky-panky if it would have contributed significantly to Blossom's career, but she knew that in my case it hardly would.

"We're getting there," I said.

"Yes," she said, her eyes tungsten. "Well, go right ahead—don't mind me."

Cora, who must have borne Blossom early, was not yet forty and still slim-figured, but the slimness, like everything else about her, had hard edges. Two cordlike lines had formed at each corner of her mouth, probably from working her phony smile too often. She'd bleached her hair into an approximation of Blossom's shade, but, perhaps from too much bleach, its texture had become wiry and synthetic. She wore a knitted top with sequins on it and big plastic bracelets in pastel colors.

"George is really helping, Mom," said Blossom. "The way he says things I really dig them. Even better than when Joel tells me how to read the lines."

"Good," said Cora. "You listen to George. Just don't—" and here she inserted a brassy laugh—"just don't fall in love with him."

"But I *do* love George," said Blossom, her laugh much more genuine. She patted my hand. "It's just like he was my uncle or something."

"Thanks a bunch," I said. "I have to end up the uncle. Uncles are like those second heroes Ronald Reagan used to play. The ones that never got the girl in the end."

Cora, still forcing her smile, busied her hands rearranging the flowers in a vase on the little hotel desk across from us. "I know," she said. "George is everybody's uncle, aren't you, George? I really feel safe when you're with Blossom. She's so affectionate—so trusting—that some men try to take advantage of her. I'd hate to, you know, see anything happen to ruin her career. It took such a long time to get her where she is now—a lot of work; a lot of sacrifice."

Mischief twinkled in Blossom's green eyes. "Cheer up, Mom. You'll soon be able to afford a Calvin Klein hair shirt."

"Blossom, you shouldn't talk like that. You're not a big movie star yet, you know. We've both got a long way to go."

"Relax, Cora," I said, trying to smooth it over. Being an uncle again. "Blossom's going to be fine. Everything's going to be just fine." And to myself I thought: *I hope*.

I had to take my spirit then, or essence, or astral body, or whatever you want to call it, and detach it, like in a science-fiction movie. I had to pretend that it was floating around, at another location, where I wasn't physically present. Mike Corby told me later in great detail what he'd been up to, so I almost felt I was with him, taking it all in.

With only a dim idea of what he was looking for, Mike wandered into *El Pichon Azul*, the town's most popular cantina, not far from the hotel. Jennifer Schwartz had already told us that Trish Wainwright had spent a lot of time there, and now we'd learned that it had also been one of Wally Demarest's favorite hangouts. That wasn't much of a link between the two victims, but at the moment it was the only link of any kind.

It was siesta time when Mike strolled in out of the hot, dusty sun and into the cooler interior of the fairly large establishment—much like any cabaret anywhere—with its bar, tables, dance floor, and musty daytime smell, an odor that seems to get masked by tobacco and alcohol fumes in such places at night. In the early afternoon, there weren't any patrons. In Mexico you sleep away these hottest hours of the day, return to work, and go out for entertainment late in the evening. In most bistros things don't really start jumping till close to midnight.

Mike blinked a few times to get his eyes used to the dimmer light, then continued, with his rolling bantamcock walk, to the bar. A woman was behind it, polishing glasses. In movies, bartenders are always polishing glasses. In real life, too.

"Cerveza, por favor," said Mike.

"One beer, coming up," she said in plain American English, and with a little smile. Mike took a second and closer look at her.

She was, he guessed, in her early thirties, and what you would call very attractive rather than stunningly beautiful. Sometimes, in Hollywood, this makes a woman stand out from all the standard stunningly beautiful ingenues all around. Her sandy hair was in a wind-ruffled cut she probably did herself; she wore a checked blouse and a pair of stretch slacks off somebody's rack.

As she began to draw Mike's beer from the tap, he said, "You're American."

"Yes," she said. "And I guess the next question is: What am I doing here?"

"I was going to get to that," said Mike, laughing.

She joined his laugh. "You'll be asking for a long story if you do. Maybe yours is shorter. What are *you* doing here?"

"Fapping around," said Mike. "Killing time. I'm with the motion picture they're making. Or maybe you already guessed that."

"The minute you walked in." She slid his beer toward him. "You're Mike Corby. I saw you in a couple of films. The dialogue was dubbed in and you were speaking Spanish. We get everything late here, but it all comes eventually. My name's Meredy Ames."

"How do," said Mike. "Sounds like you're a permanent fixture here. Mexican husband—is that it?"

"Sly way to work it in," she said. "I'm not married. Not any more, that is. How about you?"

"Divorced," said Mike. "Isn't everybody?"

54

"Seems that way sometimes," said Meredy. "The game of wedlock has become musical chairs. I keep busy and don't miss it."

"Just tending bar keeps you busy?"

"That and all the daily chores, like fetching bottled water or trying to find a tender chicken. Bartending's a job, which a lot of people here don't have. It keeps body and soul together."

Mike nodded and sipped his beer. "I don't want to pry, but there's got to be more to it than just that."

"That means you *do* want to pry," said Meredy, grinning. "Yes, there's more. A lot more. I don't know if I ought to tell it all to a cop, like yourself."

"*Ex*-cop," corrected Mike.

"You're quite sure?"

"Completely ex. Why? Don't tell me you're on the ten-most-wanted list or something?"

"No . . . but I am, I guess you could say, on the lam."

"Maybe I better have another beer," said Mike.

"Fine," she said. "And since things are this slow, I'll have one with you."

They moved from the bar and sat at a table.

As Mike, a good listener, listened, she gave the rest of it out in bits and pieces. He had already sensed that a mutual attraction had sprung up between them, and he had an idea that when they got around to comparing their likes and dislikes—an exercise, he now felt, that was bound to take place before long—they'd find a lot of things in common. It goes that way sometimes when people first meet, and if it does it's sensed right from the beginning.

"Clarence," she said. "I was married to a man named Clarence. He was very smooth and even sort of handsome. Good company most of the time. He seemed to know a little bit about everything. Glib—I guess that's the word."

At first, Meredy had known only vaguely that Clarence was "in business." Even when she began to detect faintly shady practices, she still thought of it as business.

55

In her then naive way she told herself that in business everybody bent the truth a little once in a while. Clarence was always hopping from one enterprise to the next. Tickets for phony charity affairs sold over the phone ... desert plots as home sites ... fake sweepstakes that never paid off ... expensive bibles the deceased hadn't really ordered.

He was always looking for the one big score that never came.

"By the time I realized Clarence was a bunco artist," she said, "it was too late. I mean I was so used to it by then I no longer batted an eye at it. I couldn't think of Clarence as a criminal. He didn't think of himself as one."

"Bunco artists never do," said Mike, shrugging.

"Anyway," she continued, "Clarence finally went too far. He got into a fencing operation with a gang of truck hijackers—it was more like brokering than fencing. They'd lift the stuff and Clarence would find buyers for it. One day the hijackers got into a shootout and killed somebody, and that made everything more visible. By the time they tracked the operation down to Clarence's part in it, they were in a mood to throw the book at him—which they did."

"And you got hit by the same book?"

She sighed and nodded. "Clarence had a business front. I handled the office. I also, I must admit, had full knowledge of what was going on. I was indicted right along with him."

"Look," said Mike, "I don't know the details, but it sounds like something a good lawyer could have handled easily."

"Oh, I had a good enough lawyer. He wanted me to cop a plea and testify against Clarence even if I was his wife. I wouldn't do it. He said I was facing a stiff jail sentence in that case—the D.A. and the judge were on a big civic cleanup campaign—but I still wouldn't do it."

"You were too much in love with Clarence, then."

"That's the funny thing. I wasn't. Hadn't been for some time. With all his charm and persuasiveness in the beginning, Clarence had worked a kind of scam on *me,* but the magic spell had worn off by this time. We were about to call it splits when the boom got lowered. I was mixed up, you see...scared, mixed up, not knowing which way to turn."

"So then what happened?"

"I jumped bail. Came here to Chirapulco. There used to be an art school here and I'd gone to it for a few months—that's how I knew about the place. Then there was the divorce, slipped into all of this somewhere, and what it all adds up to is that now Clarence is in the slammer, and I'm here."

"What about extradition?"

"It just hasn't caught up with me. I guess they're all busy with other things by this time. But if I returned to the States, I'd always be wondering if some accident wouldn't put me right back where I was. I couldn't live with that."

Mike blew foam. He'd lost count of his beers. "So now does it just go on like this forever?"

"I don't know." She was frowning, looking into the air rather than at Mike. "I need time. To think. Lots of time. I'm waiting for the daze to go away, which it doesn't seem to do. Meanwhile, it's not too bad here. I tend bar, keep house, and paint a lot. When I was young I thought I'd be a great artist someday. I don't know now if I'm even good, let alone great. Just doing it is enough for the time being."

"I'll have to confess I'm not too much into art," said Mike. "But I can always look and learn. When do I get to see your stuff?"

"Anytime," she said with a sudden smile. "In fact, I'll be off work pretty soon...."

Mike and Meredy, unhampered by their clothes now, lay side by side on the old-fashioned brass bed in the one big room that was both her pad and studio. There were

57

painted gourds, multicolored ears of corn, and serapes and bullfight posters on the walls. Her easel, on which stood a work in progress, was in the middle of the room, and a dozen paintings she'd already finished were either hung or propped against the walls here and there.

It was that delightful, tender time just after they'd made love; the pad, with its thick adobe walls, was cooler than the outside, which baked in the afternoon sun, but it was still warm enough within to make their bodies glisten with moisture. Meredy's body, Mike learned to his delight, was essentially slim, but gently rounded wherever it changed shape. Her breasts, their nipples centered in large maroon disks, lay slightly flattened, like Jell-O on a plate.

From where he rested, Mike could see some of the paintings. The colors were vivid, he thought, and he could recognize the people and the Mexican backgrounds depicted, but the shapes were manipulated so that there were bold lines and striking angles.

"They look good to me," he said, "but that may not mean much. I've been told I have lousy taste."

Meredy laughed. "Well, you're honest about it. That's the beginning of good taste right there."

He studied her smile for a moment, then said, "I'm not always honest, either."

"Who is?"

"Don't interrupt. This is a confession. I didn't just wander into the bar today to kill time. I was hoping to pump somebody—you, as it turned out—for information."

"About what?"

"You heard about Trish Wainwright, I suppose." He saw her nod. "I'm sort of looking into it. And that's confidential, by the way. I understand Trish used to hang out in the Blue Pigeon. Did you know her?"

"Not intimately," said Meredy. "But, yes, I did see her fairly often. Talked to her a few times, the way a bartender does. What do you want to know, anyway?"

"I'm not sure. Just fishing. What was the big attraction for her at the cantina? Anybody particular she hung around with?"

"That's easy. Ernesto Mendoza y Villasenor—or Ernie, as she called him."

"Who he?"

"The town's top political boss. Nice-looking guy. Gray at the temples—aristocratic. Ernie's got a wife back at his hacienda, but I guess she's turning to fat or something. Anyway, Trish and Ernie enjoyed each other, and, as far as I was concerned, it was their business."

"Okay," said Mike. "Now, what about Wally Demarest? You must have seen him around, too."

"The stunt man? That was a terrible accident." There was a beat as a new thought struck her. "Don't tell me it wasn't—"

"I'm not sure. Wally may have been doped before he jumped. For now, I'd like to know who *he* hung around with."

"I feel like some old biddy gossiping over the back fence," said Meredy, with a frown. "But I guess it's important, so here goes. Wally was gay—did you know that?"

Mike nodded. "He didn't hide it. Didn't push it, but didn't hide it, either."

"So is our premier bullfighter in these parts, which makes him not much of a bullfighter in other parts. Quiet, nice-looking lad. He has a last name somewhere, but everybody calls him *El Alacrán*—the Scorpion. From the way he stings the bulls I suppose. Anyway, this little love affair between Wally and his bullfighter was kept quite discreet. All they did was meet in the Blue Pigeon and have a drink together once in a while. I mean, that's all they did in public. I liked both of them and whatever they did in private was their business, as far as I'm concerned." She stretched deliciously in the bed. "But I don't suppose all this has anything to do with how Wally died."

"Possibly not." Mike shrugged. "It's just that I have

to get the background before I can even start thinking about an investigation."

"Are you thinking about it now?"

"Not really."

"Good," said Meredy, rolling to her side and pressing herself into him. "It's such a lovely afternoon. It'd be a shame to waste it just thinking. . . ."

CHAPTER SIX

As Mike, almost without realizing it, began to drift into what amounted to an investigation, Lance Haverford seemed to wake up to the hard reality that he was way behind schedule and way over budget. He started to shoot more pages per day than he had when operating in his usual perfectionist fashion. That's how shooting progress is measured: by pages of script. In TV movies you go fast—conceivably as much as twelve pages a day. In theater presentations it may be two, three, or even a fraction of a page. Nearly everybody prefers the slower pace, which gives you more time to sink your teeth into whatever you're doing. At any rate, the accelerated pace now kept me busy and gave me less time to wonder about what progress Mike might be making.

There was occasional discussion, of course, of the two tragic deaths, one clearly a murder, and the other apparently an accident, with only Mike and myself thinking it might not be. While Roberta Vale and I were waiting for a scene we had together, I talked it over with her.

Although Roberta Vale tends to be a scene-stealer, she's great to work with. Her magnificence rubs off on you, and you find yourself doing better than you thought you could. We sat on camp chairs in the shade of the honey wagon, enjoying what had become a rare treat— two glasses of plain ice water.

We were both in costume, and the frontier garb she wore gave her an unexpected grandeur, or maybe it was the other way around. Roberta was still slim; her figure never had become matronly. In her youth, she'd been compared to Katherine Hepburn and Bette Davis; she was still, in many ways, a combination of these two great artists.

"The trouble with show business," she said, in her faintly southern accent, "is that it now costs too much money. There was a day when a good story could be told by leaving many details to the imagination. Now, everything has to be meticulously authentic and photographically real. At ten times the expense. A hundred times."

"Well, I think I see what you mean," I said. "But we *are* in the business of creating illusions. Seems to me anything we can do to make those illusions more convincing is all to the good."

Years ago, at the height of her popularity, Roberta had walked out of the acting profession, baffling everyone by saying she simply didn't care to do it any longer. Lance Haverford, who had probably seen every old movie ever made, had located her somewhere in the depths of Alabama, about half of which her family owned, and had talked her into reappearing in *The Godless*.

"The illusions," she said, "need not be created with so much emphasis on the technical aspect. So much that the dramatic values are overwhelmed by it."

I smiled. "You sound like Peter Revelstoke now."

She smiled. "He's a bit of a shit, isn't he?"

There is nothing like the impact of a four-letter word delivered in a completely cultivated and aristocratic accent.

"Today it's all dollars and cents," she said. "Hardly anyone starts out to make a superb picture. They start out to make box-office smashes. If it also turns into a great movie, that's almost beside the point."

I shrugged. "It was that way in the old days, too. I still think *The Godless* may become a great film we can all be artistically proud of."

"If it ever gets shown."

"Well," I admitted, "there are some budget problems—"

"More than that." Her frown, like all of her expressions, was restrained—even elusive. "I have a strange feeling that certain forces are out to destroy this effort— to keep it from ever reaching the screen. It's intuitive, and there's not much in the way of hard fact to back it up, but I swear there's a vibration of hostility in the air. It's become especially strong since Trish was murdered and Wally had his accident. I keep wondering, who's against us? God himself? Doesn't He like the title of this movie? Is it that simple?"

I laughed. "Don't look for disaster, Roberta. You do that, and sometimes you find it."

"George," she said, "I will be very happy if what I say turns out to be no more than the wild imaginings of the dotty old lady I've become."

While this renewed effort on the shooting of the picture was taking place, Mike, who wasn't on call, kept busy with his still somewhat off-the-cuff investigation. Maybe he used it primarily as an excuse to hang around *El Pichon Azul* and see more of Meredy. Since he told me everything in detail later, I think I can reconstruct what happened to him there with a certain amount of accuracy.

It was late afternoon and all the denizens of Chirapulco were emerging from their siestas, like cockroaches coming out of the walls.

Meredy was busy serving customers who had just wandered in, and Mike was in a far corner of the room, casually trying to question one of the cooks in his fair-to-middlin' Spanish about the activities of Trish Wainwright and Wally Demarest when they'd visited the establishment. There was what amounted to a sudden silence, and heads began to turn toward the front door. Mike looked in that direction, too.

From Meredy's previous description, Mike knew that the man who had just entered was Ernesto Mendoza y Villasenor, or, as Trish had fondly called him, "Ernie." He wore an immaculate white pleated shirt outside his

63

trousers—I forget what they call them, but I always buy a few when I'm in Mexico—and in it he looked as formal as though he'd dressed for a wedding. He was handsome, every inch an aristocrat, and there was only a faint suggestion of wolfishness in his finely cut features.

Ernie had a small retinue with him. The man on his right looked like a squat stone figure retrieved from some Yucatán archaeological site, and the man on his left was bulky and walleyed. I don't know what it is about Mexico, but exotropia seems widespread there. Maybe they have to look two ways on account of the traffic. Anyway, this was the Mexican version of a tableau Mike had seen before. The boss and his torpedoes.

Ernie, pausing only a moment at the door to survey the dimmer interior, stalked across the room directly toward Mike. He halted a few feet from him and showed a cold smile.

"Good afternoon, Senor Corby," he said. "I am Ernesto Mendoza y Villasenor. I think you must have heard of me. I think you must have heard a great many things which are not really your concern. It is an American custom to come to the point quickly, and that is what I shall do now."

Mike showed him a poker face. "Okay, senor," he said. "What point?"

"Perhaps you do not intend to be rude, but I'm afraid all the questions you've been asking about certain private affairs here in Chirapulco are exactly that. Apparently you wish to investigate the very sad killing of Senorita Wainwright. It is not your job, senor, and it stirs up too much rumor and bad feeling. I must ask you to stop your efforts at once. It would be well if you do not ever return to this cantina."

"Is that so?" Mike took a bulldog stance, with his legs spread a little. "Well, senor, I'm afraid I can't oblige you. In fact, what you say makes me just a little more inclined to look a little deeper into this whole bucket of worms."

"I was afraid that would be your position," said Ernie,

as though sighing. He glanced at the stone figure on his right. "Pepe." And then at the walleyed man on his left. "Bernardo."

That was all it took—the quiet mention of their names.

They sprang forward, and Mike had just enough time to see them coming. Pepe lowered his head and charged like a bull. Bernado, from the other side, swung a looping arm as though he were delivering a blow with a cudgel.

Mike managed to duck the punch, but couldn't get out of Pepe's way. Pepe crashed into him, encircled him with his heavy arms, and tried to throw him down and to one side. As Mike put it later, barroom brawling is an international art and whatever is effective in a New York alley does just as well in a Mexican cantina. He brought his knee up into Pepe's groin. Pepe grunted a little—though not as much as Mike had expected—and his grip loosened just enough for Mike to twist himself out of it.

By this time the other customers in the joint had their eyes glued, half-fascinated, on this sudden entertainment. Some stared blankly; others smiled nervously.

It's impossible for me to relay to you, from Mike's account of the episode, a blow-by-blow description, but it was evidently quite a dance, with Mike deftly eluding frontal attacks, then prancing this way and that to get in his own return blows. He didn't elude everything. One of the problems was that he couldn't read Bernardo's walleyes to see where he intended to strike next. From both men, a number of kicks and punches landed squarely—once Mike was dazed and thought he'd go down, but managed to stay on his legs until they were no longer rubbery.

In movie fights contact is not made, the camera angle concealing this, and the sound of knuckles striking flesh is dubbed in later. In real fights the knuckles get as much damage as the flesh they strike. I wish they'd show this in a movie sometime—but it would probably slow up the story.

There was no way for Mike to measure the time that was passing, though the whole thing couldn't have been much more than a matter of seconds. There was a moment at last when Mike began to suspect that he was going to be dropped. He hoped he'd retain enough consciousness, when he hit the floor, to roll himself up like an armadillo so their kicks wouldn't find too many soft spots.

At this juncture there was a sudden bustling at the front door. Mike sensed it only vaguely. The next thing he knew, four khaki-clad policemen were separating Mike from his attackers, and them from him, and, moments later, still breathing hard, he was looking up into the ripe-olive eyes of Alfonso Cruz, the *capitano de descrubimientos*.

"Glad you got here," said Mike, finding difficulty in panting out even those few words.

"We will talk," said Cruz impassively. "In my office."

The office was seedy—a tiny cubicle filled with old, scarred furniture—but since New York City police offices are also pretty much that way Mike felt almost at home.

Cruz lit a foul-smelling cigarette. "Now," he said. "I have learned many things. It has come to my attention that you took a certain beverage drunk by Senor Demarest before his accident to Los Angeles, where it was examined for toxic substance, no?"

"That's right," said Mike. "It was loaded with barbiturates. I think they threw Wally's timing way off and caused the accident. Or even killed him directly. It could have been murder."

"In that case, why did you not express your suspicions to me?"

"Because they were only that. Suspicions. Nothing in the way of hard evidence."

"And you decided to look for better evidence?"

"Yes. Anything wrong with that?"

"There is everything wrong with that, Senor Corby,"

said Cruz, his voice steel under velvet—the *estoque* draped by the *muleta* just before the kill. "*I* am investigating this case," he said. "In my own way. I am looking quite thoroughly into the deaths of both Senorita Wainwright and Senor Demarest. It interferes to have anyone else do the same without my knowledge. It is also illegal, in my country as in yours, to withhold evidence. I should think that you, as a former policeman, would realize this."

"Okay," said Mike. "Maybe I was a little out of line. I intended to bring you anything in the way of a firm lead if I happened to dig one up. It's your squeal, captain. I'm not trying to take it away from you."

"I hope not, senor," said Cruz. "Let me tell you right now that I mean to close both of these cases and not only because that is my job. If I am ever to be transferred to *El Capital*, where I much prefer to be, I will need to attract favorable notice. The murder of Senorita Wainwright presents just such an opportunity. I would not care to have it thought in Mexico City that I needed the assistance of some gringo policeman."

Mike shook his head. "You've got it all wrong, captain. Even if I should break the case, the credit would be all yours. The only thing I want is to have whoever killed Miss Wainwright—and Wally Demarest, if he was murdered—collared."

"Perhaps," said Cruz, thinking it over for a moment. "Unfortunately, senor, you are something of a celebrity, and most people will believe you solved the case—if you take part in the investigation. But there is more to this. Your interference disturbs my own plans of investigation."

"Oh? How come?"

"For one example, Senor Mendoza y Villasenor is now alerted because of your efforts. I meant to look into his possible connection with the case in a much quieter way. He is a wealthy man, from a distinguished family, and quite powerful here. He can do much to block an investigation if, by any chance, it threatens him. In short, Senor Corby, I must ask you to step aside completely."

"Well, now," Mike said thoughtfully, "I can't just ignore any evidence or suspicions I happen to run into. And I don't think you have any legal grounds to keep me from asking a few questions here and there."

Cruz smiled dryly. "For that, senor," he said, "I don't need legal grounds."

Mike reported all this to me the next day as we rode out to location in the same sedan.

"You gonna lay off, like Cruz says?" I asked.

"I don't know," said Mike, frowning. "Depends on what you mean by 'lay off.' And what Cruz means. Also what I mean."

"And what *do* you mean?"

"Don't know that, either," said Mike. "At least, not yet."

After breakfast and costuming and makeup, and after all the usual preparations on the set, from lighting to a careful check of all the props, I got ready with Blossom Foster for a scene we were to play together.

Yul Brynner was also in it. He wasn't in the main cast—he'd been flown in for a cameo appearance. About a day's work. While Joel Totterelli was setting up a camera angle for the first take, I ambled up to Yul, who stood there dressed as a Mexican peon, with a serape over his shoulder and a huge Jalisco sombrero on his head.

"Where you been lately, Yul? Haven't seen you around."

"That's where I've been. Around," he said with a quiet smile.

He never gives out information about himself. He's got to be the most private guy in Hollywood. I guess it adds to his air of mystery, which is one of his bankable assets.

Jennifer Schwartz, her clipboard hard against her

breast, came up to us, looking around anxiously. "Where's Lance?"

"Damned if I know," I said.

Joel Totterelli heard that and turned. "We don't need Lance. Let's get started."

"He left strict instructions," said Jennifer, frowning.

"Okay." Joel sighed a little. "Somebody find Lance. We'll take a quick walk-through. It won't hurt him to miss that."

Joel blocked out the scene as we all listened, smiling when we understood what he was after. Jennifer had scuttled off to locate Lance. The whole scene was for the sake of what amounted to a visual gag, to be thrown in as a cutaway, as a transition from one important plot scene to the next. It would save a dissolve from one scene to the next to indicate a passage of time, and anytime you can avoid an optical, which always calls attention to itself, the story moves along that much more smoothly.

In the story I, as the fire chief, was always getting the barber to rub a special tonic on my head so I wouldn't lose my hair. Blossom and I, walking along, would be discussing this, and I, seeing a peon sitting against a wall and sunning himself, would say something about Mexicans being lucky and never getting bald. There would then be a close-up of the peon, his big hat shading his face. He'd remove the hat and raise his head slowly, and turn out to be Yul Brynner, whom everyone would recognize. It was another example of Lance's profligacy; it couldn't be just some bald extra—it had to be Yul Brynner, at his prices.

In the midst of the walk-through, Jennifer came scrambling back toward us, stumbling over everything. Her eyes were wide, her face was pale, and her breasts were bouncing because she didn't even have her clipboard with her.

"Lance!" she cried, her voice breaking. "In the honey wagon!"

Joel looked at her in faint annoyance. "What about Lance?"

69

"You look!" she gasped. "Go there and look!"

She broke into tears and couldn't speak.

We rushed to the honey wagon. I don't know who got there first. When I barged in I saw Lance, flat on his back, arms outflung, on the floor of one of the dressing rooms.

His eyes, still and staring, were like the marbles we used to call realies when I was a kid. His skin seemed fish-belly white where it wasn't covered by his dark, spaded beard.

There was a bluish bullet-hole almost dead center in his forehead.

CHAPTER SEVEN

"Good evening one and all."

That was how Peter Revelstoke always began his broadcasts, and I'd had a transcript made of this one.

"Death hangs over the set of *The Godless,* the highly-touted, but pedestrian, production-line western now being filmed on location in Mexico.

"Lance Haverford, its producer, once hailed as a young genius, was found shot, with a 32-caliber bullet between the eyes, in a trailer on the set, while the filming was taking place. The identity of his assailant is at present unknown. The identity of the murderer of socially prominent Trish Wainwright, who died on the same location, is still unknown. And now I have learned—and this is exclusive—that Mexican authorities believe the death of stunt man Wally Demarest, in a fall from a cliff, was not —repeat, not—accidental. He may have been drugged, causing him to lose his balance during the stunt."

At this point, Revelstoke paused and gave the camera a smug, I-told-you-so look.

Then he continued.

"Those who are superstitious believe this motion picture is jinxed. I predict that there will be walkouts on the set. Others suspect that divine punishment may be at work as a warning against the moral degradation that surrounded this cinematic effort from the beginning.

"I am saddened, as anyone must be, by the deaths of all three victims, but my main concern is with the artistic merit of the production itself. There is very little of that in spite of the huge sums of money that have gone into it.

"So there is another sadness here. If someone is committing murder because of this motion picture it is a wasted effort. It is like murdering a sick patient who is going to die anyway. Murder is never excusable, of course, no matter what the circumstances. It is just that in this case it is particularly sordid and, in addition to being immoral, illegal, and shocking, is in an even higher degree of bad taste.

"But that's Hol-l-lywood for you. . . ."

"The schmuck," said Ira Yoder.

He perched, sparrowlike, on a chair next to mine in the hotel's banquet room where we had all gathered for the conference Phyllis Upton had called. Folding chairs had been set up and it resembled a small stockholder's meeting. The entire company was on hand, and we were waiting for Phyllis to appear.

"Agreed," I said to Ira. "But I thought you said the only bad publicity is no publicity at all."

"That's right," said Ira. "And this isn't bad publicity. It'll pack 'em in. The same ones who watch Indianapolis, hoping the cars'll crash. Revelstoke's still a schmuck. Any publicity he gives us, good or bad, won't mean a thing if the picture never gets finished. Which, it looks like now, it won't."

Phyllis now bustled in from the rear of the room, accompanied by Joel Totterelli, who looked a little pale, and by the ubiquitous Jennifer Schwartz, who this time carried a stack of papers instead of a clipboard. There was a lectern up front, and when Phyllis took her place behind it she assumed a kind of commanding presence that largely overcame her warthog appearance.

"Ladies and gentlemen," she said, swinging her eyes over all of us, "I first want to thank you all for coming here, and I want to express my grief and dismay over what happened to Lance Haverford. I understand that a memorial service is being planned, and I, along with many of you, will be paying respects there."

We shifted in our seats. There was what amounted to a group sigh.

"But this is a business meeting," said Phyllis, "and here we will deal with business. As it has often been said, the show must go on. That is the first announcement to answer the question you must all have in your minds. We will continue with the shooting of the picture."

At any other time there would have been applause, but with the hush of death still hanging over us there was only a stirring as we traded glances with our neighbors. We were pleased and relieved at what we'd heard, but it wasn't seemly to express pleasure.

"In the past twenty-four hours," continued Phyllis, "I have been in close and constant communication with the financial interests behind the production of *The Godless*. I have copies of the basic messages, which Ms. Schwartz will pass out to you, so that you are all fully informed. As one of our principal backers, Mr. J. Sutton Fargo has made the decisions which the bank officers and other interested parties have agreed to. I would like to announce now that I am to take over the producer's chores for the remainder of the shooting."

We stirred in our seats again. In the looks that were exchanged, I could see none of doubt or objection. Most of us felt that Phyllis would be quite competent. There was precedent for this sort of thing in, for example, the way Joan Harrison, Alfred Hitchcock's executive producer, did much of the work on some of his films and later became a producer in her own right. And it may even have been that some of us felt a secret relief at the prospect of no longer having to endure many of Lance's tyrannies.

"Unfortunately," said Phyllis, "we are not yet quite out of the woods. Mr. Fargo agreed to continue with some reluctance. In fact, I had all I could do to persuade him. And we are still faced with the problem of a cost overrun, with Mr. Fargo as our only possible source of funds to meet it. We are borrowed dry elsewhere."

Ira whispered to me, "Ain't everybody?" I shushed him.

"Meanwhile," said Phyllis, "I will make an attempt to shoot more economically, hoping that we can somehow catch up with the budget. It will mean cutting corners. This will require your cooperation in helping us to finish all the footage as quickly as possible with a minimum of setup and rehearsal time and with the fewest possible retakes. You are all skilled professionals, and I know you can do it."

The looks we gave each other this time said, "Hell, yes, we can do it."

"There is one more thing to keep in mind." Phyllis's eyes drifted back and forth as she sought the right words for what she had to say. They looked like the eyes of a bullfrog ready to lasso an insect with its tongue. "Mr. Fargo, as some of you may know, has rather rigid moral standards. Every breath of scandal makes him less and less inclined to continue his support. Two murders— possibly three—have already given him thoughts of withdrawing. We must avoid offending him if the picture is to be finished. I don't like this any more than you do, but we must all be very careful about our personal affairs until we wrap up here on location."

There were frowns. Nobody likes to be told to behave, especially when he or she is behaving anyway.

"The murders have dramatized everything," Phyllis said. "They've drawn too much attention to us. It might help if they could be solved; with the blame put where it belongs the suspicion of depravity would fall from the rest of us. At any rate, that's where we stand. Frankly, not in a very good position. But if we roll up our sleeves, get to work, and have a little good luck for a change, I think we can finish this picture. It's up to all of us. . . ."

At the table in the cantina, Mike and I sipped beer. Very slowly. Those around us imbibed their own drinks

74

the same way that evening—somberly and without the slightest air of revelry.

I think for many of the cast and crew members, the reaction hadn't quite set in yet. The way they were thinking—or feeling, if that's more like it—was in the air and you could feel it. Here we'd had three unexplained deaths in a row, two of them obviously murder, and they weren't in the least expected or allowed for according to normal probabilities, and, what was more, they seemed completely disconnected from each other and without reason. The whole thing was just a little too far-out to believe and everybody was a little stunned by it—almost as though momentarily ignoring it in the hope that it was an illusion and would soon go away.

I hesitate to lay claim to any prescience—though I've always been fascinated by the psychic and the occult—but after Lance's murder I had an elusive idea about all three killings tugging at my subconscious mind. Since there didn't seem to be any reason for anyone to kill three such victims in a row, I wondered if there *had* to be a reason. The killer—if there was one and only one—could be motivated by madness and nothing more; there had been many such killings down through the ages and there will probably be more as time goes on. In which case, I theorized, an investigator would not be looking so much for a motive as for signs of flakiness that would enable someone to murder without much motive. I recognized this as a somewhat unprofessional theory even as it came to me, so, at the time, I didn't mention it to Mike Corby. I didn't know he was already thinking along the same lines—at least vaguely.

But that was not how he started off the discussion. "George," he said thoughtfully, "do you read Phyl the way I do? Did she say it would help if I could find out who knocked off Trish and Wally and Lance?"

"Something like that," I said. "I think she was hoping that the Mexican authorities would get to the bottom of it—not you especially."

"I don't think they will," said Mike. "Cruz probably

75

knows his stuff, but he hasn't got much in the way of facilities."

"Have you?"

"Well, not exactly, but I have some contacts that might help."

"Like those you used to get the poison analyzed?"

"Like that. And now, the silencer."

I wrinkled my brows. "What silencer?"

"There had to be one. When Lance was shot. It's the only answer."

"I don't think I follow you."

"Look," said Mike. "Lance was shot in the honey wagon while the scene was being blocked out on the set. Now, the wagon isn't that far from the set. Someone would have heard an ordinary shot. The fact that a silencer was used tells us something. It could narrow things down."

"How?"

"Okay," said Mike, "I'll lay it out for you. The slug was 32-caliber—I got that from the doc, who was in on the autopsy. Most likely a handgun; most likely an automatic. The powder tattoo on the forehead shows he got it from only a few feet away. From somebody who could get close enough to use a handgun. That suggests somebody who knew Lance—maybe even somebody who could arrange to meet him in the honey wagon."

"Somebody in the cast or crew? Is that what you're saying?"

"Probably. All this is probable, not necessarily absolutely true. Meanwhile, the silencer—if there was one—might give us a good lead."

"How do you figure that?"

"A silencer," said Mike, "is a very unusual item. It's close to impossible for the average citizen to get one. They're procured through shady dealers in only a few big cities. Anybody who gets a silencer is leaving a visible trail—much more visible than just picking up a handgun somewhere. Now, let's assume somebody in our production company made the right connections and got

76

one. Maybe through one of these outfits that specializes in procuring props—they can dig up almost anything. Chances are overwhelming it was done in the Los Angeles area. It wouldn't be at all a waste of time to poke around there. Some of my buddies at LAPD could steer me to some of these dealers."

"But would the dealers talk?"

"Maybe. Maybe not. People like that like to suck up to cops, and sometimes they don't give a damn about snitching on their customers. Like drug dealers who make a standard practice of informing for the usual ten percent on any bust. Anyway, it's how I'd start if I had jurisdiction and a staff to do some of the legwork."

"You wanna go to L.A. and try?"

"Thinking about it. Several people are flying back over the weekend. I could slip in without letting them know what I'm doing. Unless you happen to be flying in, too."

"Better take the jet," I said. "Flying with me wouldn't leave you enough time. As a matter of fact," I said, shifting my rump as the thought hit me, "I wouldn't mind tagging along with you to see what you do. If I wouldn't be in the way."

Mike grinned. "It's always good to have a partner. Even if he is a rank amateur...."

All airplanes fascinate me, but especially jets. If I had more time—and, of course, more money—I'd be checked out in jets, or, dream of dreams, own one. I tell you this to explain why I readily took the copilot's seat on the way to Los Angeles even if it did mean putting up with Ferdinand Holtz for a while. Ferdy was glad to have a rated pilot beside him. I could do things like handle the radio and watch out for traffic.

The other passengers, including Mike, were back in the cabin space, entertaining themselves in various ways. Phyllis and Joel were going over the script, trying to decide where they could save money. Cora Foster was reading a paperback romance and worrying about Blos-

77

som, whom she'd left alone with the wolves—a wolf, to her, being any normal, red-blooded male. Ira Yoder was pecking out publicity releases on a small portable typewriter. Grande Dame Roberta Vale was beating Jennifer Schwartz at game after game of gin rummy—gleefully, even though they were only playing for quarters.

All the sky in the world slammed toward us and fell swiftly behind. Through the broken clouds below, we watched the slower moving endless brown nothing of the landscape.

Ferdy looked at home in a cockpit, the way some cowboys look at home on a horse. He was a short, tough little man with a balding head, bright blue eyes, and a rolling bantam swagger. They must have had his kind in the old Luftwaffe in World War II, a special breed, I think, just made for the Messerschmidts. He had come to America in his teens some twenty years ago, and, with tremendous energy, and with the self-discipline that often seems a part of Germanic culture, had bootstrapped himself up from the status of a penniless immigrant to that of a sought-after private pilot.

"Nice day for flying," I said.

He nodded. "*Ja*. But I think maybe too easy. Nothing to do but sit here."

"I suppose I could work up a screaming emergency for you if you really want one," I said dryly.

"You know what I mean. All straight and level. Like driving a bus. I think sometimes I would rather be a test pilot. Or a fighter pilot. That would be even better. Too bad we don't have a good war somewhere right now."

"Is there such a thing?" I asked.

"Is there what, such a thing?"

"A good war."

"Of course there is. It is natural that in a war people get hurt and killed. But the strongest ones survive and that makes the whole country stronger. Every great nation in the world, including the United States, of which I am now a loyal citizen, has a history of wars."

"I can't believe the wars themselves made them great," I said, wondering why I was bothering to argue.

Ferdy shook his head. "War means progress. Always great new discoveries because the need is urgent. Medicine, for example. What we learned in recent wars now saves more lives than the wars ever took. Or science. We could not have gone to the moon if military rockets had not been developed."

"That's open to question, Ferdy."

"Look. In World War II everybody thought the V-2's were a terrible weapon. But almost the same rockets were pretty soon going out into space. Exciting days. I was born too late for them." He sighed. "I have studied that war. I don't know why Germany lost. It did everything right."

"Uh huh," I said. "But for the wrong reasons. And the wrongest reason of all was believing what you're thinking now. That war somehow produces a master race."

"Well, it does. Look how strong America became. The greatest power in the world. Now they're going down again. Russia will take over one of these days just because we're afraid to stand up to them. Do you know what's wrong with America? Instead of weeding out the cowards and weaklings it takes care of them."

"I thought that was what was right with America," I said.

Because the conversation had taken that turn, I suppose, we cut it short for a while and just sat there as the airplane, on auto-pilot, flew itself. Ferdy, no doubt, had his own thoughts to keep him company; I certainly had mine, and they were mostly about the three killings that had taken place. For a while I lost track of time, so I wasn't sure how much of it had passed before Ferdy, in the pilot's seat, made what sounded to me like a sudden, soft gasp.

I snapped my head around and stared at him. His face was strained and he had his hand pressed to his chest just below the rib cage.

"Ferdy! You okay?"

He brought his eyes around as though realizing for the first time that I was looking at him. "It's nothing!" he said abruptly. "Nothing at all!"

"Are you sure? You look like you're having some kind of pain—"

"No, no, no," he said, shaking his head rapidly. "A little indigestion, that is all. It is that Mexican food!"

"I thought you never touched it."

"Well, I did. This once," he said, almost angrily.

Maybe it was the way he became suddenly defensive about it that made me wonder; or maybe it was just my sixth sense working overtime again. "Ferdy, ordinarily this would be none of my business, but since you're flying this airplane I think maybe it is. That little stab of pain you just put up with wouldn't be something else, would it?"

"What do you mean, something else?"

"Something that might show up on your next physical. And maybe lose your commercial license for you. Something you might not even want to admit to yourself. Let's say it right out, Ferdy. Heart trouble."

He stared at me angrily for a long moment, then said, "You are crazy, George!"

"I hope I am," I said. "I hope you're as healthy as a prize bull and that you live forever."

"That is exactly what I intend to do," he said, "or something close to it."

He took the airplane off auto-pilot, grabbed the yoke, and began to fly it himself—as though to prove to me he still could.

Captain Oliver Kingsley greeted us warmly in his office in downtown L.A. Mike mumbled an introduction, and I never did catch Kingsley's exact position in the LAPD, but evidently contraband weaponry was one of his concerns. I was also a little vague about how he and Mike Corby had first met; something about a school or seminar on law enforcement they'd once attended together, but anyway they seemed to enjoy seeing each other again.

Kingsley was a tweedy pipe-smoker who didn't look like a cop. These days a lot of cops don't look like cops. Not the flatfoot kind you always used to see in B-pictures, anyway.

"Silencers, huh?" he said, after Mike had explained why he'd called upon him. "Interesting device—and all wrong the way they show them in the movies. Invented way back in 1908 by an American inventor named Hiram Maxim. It whirls the gases in a spiral till they lose speed, and that way they don't make so much noise coming out. When silencers first appeared everybody flipped and the states started passing laws against them. They thought every criminal would want one. Not so."

"Oh?" said Mike. "How come?"

"Well, to begin, they don't work on just any old gun. Not on revolvers, for example, which have a sound leak between the cylinder and the barrel. Automatics can be modified for them—it takes machine-shop work—but they work best on single-shot weapons, which most criminals don't want. The only real customer for a silencer is a professional assassin, who can do his job with one shot. Even they would rather not be limited to one shot, for the most part. And there aren't enough of them to create any kind of a mass market for silencers. So they're usually machined to order—sometimes abroad—by small, private gunsmiths, who charge an arm and a leg, and who frequently make the gun that goes with it."

"Anybody like that around here?" asked Mike.

"None I know about," said Kingsley. "But if I wanted a silencer I'd probably go to somebody like Nick Spitalny."

"Who's he?"

"On the outside, a legitimate gun dealer. Under the table, a procurer of damn near any weapon from old Thompson subs to bazookas. He supplies outfits like that underground group Patty Hearst was involved with, or, on the other side, those neo-Nazi organizations who train in camps out in the country. We know he's doing it, and the Feds know, but we've never been able to prove anything. Not enough to make a case in court, anyway. Even if we did get an indictment he'd probably wiggle out of it with a slap-on-the-wrist fine or something. There's another aspect. Spitalny's a born snitch and sometimes leads us to somebody we'd rather have than him. You know how it is."

"How it is and how it ever shall be," said Mike, with a sigh.

Later, Mike and I had dinner in a steak house that was more convenient than special; we discussed what we knew so far and failed to arrive at much we didn't know already. It had been past office hours by the time we'd finished with Captain Kingsley, so we decided to put off our call on Nick Spitalny, whose shop was somewhere in Inglewood, until the next day.

I ordered a tenderloin, medium-rare.

"What are you gonna do?" I asked Mike. "Just walk up to the guy and ask if he's sold any silencers lately, and, if so, to whom?"

"Well, not right off the bat," said Mike. "With these characters you have to beat around the bush first. I'll drop a few hints."

"Like what?"

"He's got to think he's getting something out of it before he'll talk. Like, if there was a big fat reward for somebody he'd sold an unregistered weapon to, he'd turn on him in a minute—especially if he had an understanding he wouldn't be prosecuted for the sale. But he'll also be interested in establishing a useful contact for the future. So I'll throw out a few hints that I'm investigating for somebody big. Treasury, Congress—whatever he chooses to imagine. It'll sound like I'm a good man to do a favor for, which maybe I can return at some future date when he gets his ass in a sling. No guarantees, but if anything works it'll be an approach along those lines."

I hacked at my steak. It wasn't bad but it wasn't big

enough. That's why they urge you to go to the salad bar first in these joints, so you'll fill yourself up on rabbit food and be satisfied with the bite-size steak when it comes. "I wonder if we'll have time to see this Nick Spitalny. Phyllis was saying something about leaving in the morning."

"If she does, I'll stick around and beat my way back via airline. We've got that blanket clearance Lance arranged. You go ahead back on the jet if you want to."

"No, I don't want to miss this," I said. "Anyway, let me check right now and find out exactly when they are leaving."

On the pay phone I got Jennifer Schwartz at her apartment. She was the clearing house for this sort of information. She said, "Hi, George. I was trying to get ahold of you. We'll be heading back for Chirapulco at noon."

"That's what I wanted to know," I said. "Look, Jenny, you tell Phyl that Mike and I won't show up. We'll get a commercial flight later. I don't think either of us is on call for a coupla days, so it shouldn't make any difference."

"What are you two up to, anyway?" she asked.

I laughed. "We're not shacking up with anybody, if that's what you hoped to hear."

"Why, anything like that never even crossed my mind," said Jennifer, all righteous about it. "In fact, I can guess what you're up to. Looking into those murders, right?"

"I guess you could call it that. Mike's got a line on the weapon Lance was killed with. He thinks a silencer was used and he's poking around to see where somebody would get one." The moment I spoke I decided I shouldn't have. Me and my big mouth. We've bumped into each other before. "Uh—Jenny—keep this under your hat, okay?" Mike had asked me the same thing with the barbiturates, employing, as I seemed to remember, the same metaphor.

"Why certainly, George. I won't tell a soul."

"I'm serious, Jenny. We don't want it to get back to Alfonso Cruz. Or the media. If the murders are never solved—which might well happen—Mike will look bad for never having solved them. Revelstoke will see to that."

"All right, George," said Jennifer. "I'll keep it under my hat, just like you say."

I frowned after I hung up. It had just come to me that Jennifer never wore a hat to keep anything under. . . .

The gun shop of Nicholas M. Spitalny was on a medium-busy street in a seedy neighborhood and on the same block with everything from video-game parlors to porn shops. Something called *Debbie's Lips Go 'Round the World* was playing at a hole-in-the-wall cinema named The Pink Pussycat.

Alleycats, black and white, lounged on corners or stalked up and down the street. Way back, when I was young, and New York City was young, and the whole damned world was young, a ghetto used to be a place people schlepped in. Now it's a place where they stalk. Where you walk in wariness, whether you're the hunter or the hunted.

The arms emporium was closed tight, with steel shutters lowered and locked in front of it. A sign said, "Open 9 to 5," and it was already past ten.

"What the hell," said Mike, looking at the steel shutters.

"Maybe it's a holiday for Spitalny," I said. "Dracula's birthday?"

Our taxi was still at the curb, the driver looking nervous at being parked in this neighborhood. Mike's eye fell upon a small black man who was leaning against a doorway next to the shop, staring at us suspiciously. Defeat and resentment were in his eyes, which were also dulled over by what might have been a recent fix. Mike stepped toward him. For a moment it looked as though he might run, but he evidently changed his mind and stayed in place.

"How you doin'?" said Mike pleasantly.

The man held his surly stare.

"Yeah," said Mike. "I'm what you think. But you got nothing to worry about. All I want is a little information." He took a five-dollar bill from his pocket. "This'll get you a nickel bag, anyway."

"Shee-yit! Nickel bag costs a dime these days."

"Okay, a dime, then. If you've got good answers."

The little man rubbed his nose and sniffed audibly. His last fix had probably been longer ago than I'd thought. "What you wanna know, honky?"

"Spitalny." Mike nodded at the gun shop. "You know him?"

"Seen him around."

"Does he usually open up late?"

"Shee-yit. He always come nine o'clock. Only not today. Guess he stayed in bed. How would I know?"

"Okay. Where's he live?"

"Don't know. It ain't around here. No honky makin' all that bread gonna live around here."

"One more question. If I wanted to get me a piece without having to sign for it, would Nick Spitalny be the one to go to?"

"Hey, man!" said the junkie. "That's heavy stuff. Don't know nothin' about it!"

Mike nodded and gave him the five-dollar bill. He reiterated his request for a ten and Mike said his answers hadn't been good enough. "Shee-yit!" said the junkie. And pocketed the money.

We returned to the taxi. The driver had a towering mop of hair something like the shako on a Buckingham Palace guardsman, and had already recognized us and asked for our autographs. For his daughter or niece or somebody. That's what they always say. We told him we wanted to get to a phone book now, and he took off, but passed several phone booths where, we all knew, any directories they'd ever had would have been lifted long ago. We finally pulled into a superdrug where Mike bought some aspirin and chewing gum and talked the pharmacist in back into letting him use his phone book. Nicholas M. Spitalny was listed at an address the taxi driver said was a good forty minutes from where we were. We told him all systems go. The meter was clacking away and pretty soon it would reach a figure that represented about what the whole vehicle was worth. Everything costs money; even playing detective.

Spitalny's house turned out to be in a neighborhood that was just on the verge of becoming sleazy, which suggested either that he wasn't as prosperous as everybody thought, or that he was merely being prudent and keeping a low profile. It was one of those minor, narrow, palm-lined residential streets invariably called "boulevards" in L.A. and its environs; the residences were all thirty-year-old cracker-boxes, some frame, some stucco. Spitalny had a small front lawn that needed mowing and a little porch in front of the house. His garbage can was at the curb, its contents already collected. A supermarket shopping cart somebody had failed to return sat on the sidewalk not far from it. Curtains were drawn over all his windows.

Mike pushed the front doorbell. We heard the chimes inside go "ding-dong!" but this was followed by silence. Mike tried again. Twice. Still no answer.

"Looks like Nick's outa town or something," said Mike.

"Maybe we should have phoned first."

Mike shook his head. "Didn't want to alert him— give him too much time to think before he saw us."

"Maybe he left for his shop while we were on the way."

Mike walked to the end of the porch and glanced at the gravel driveway beside the house. "His car's here. Must be his—personalized license plate—'Nicky S.' " He came back to the door. "Suppose we keep this from being a total loss."

"What do you mean?"

"George, I don't think you want to break the law and expose yourself to a possible B and E charge. So what I want you to do is go back to the taxi and just keep driving around the block slowly, till you see me and pick me up again. If anybody should ask later, you don't have the slightest knowledge of what I was doing."

"You're going to bust in?"

"If I am, you don't know it. I didn't say it and you don't know it."

"Oh, hell," I said. "Go ahead and do it. I'll stay with you."

"You quite sure you wanna take that risk?"

"Come on, Mike," I answered. "Let's get it over with."

Mike held his eyes on me for another moment, then nodded. As a preliminary to whatever efforts he was going to make to break in, he tried the doorknob. It turned, and the door opened. "I'll be damned," he muttered.

We went in. The interior was dim and coolish. The front door opened directly into a living room full of fairly expensive furniture, but none of it coordinated, and all of it designed to make an interior decorater shudder. The paintings on the walls were drab landscapes, the kind they have to sell by reminding you that they're done in genuine oil paint.

There was a funny smell in the house. It was in addition to the faintly musty odor of the interior, which was probably permanent. It took me a second or two to realize what it reminded me of. Something from way back in the past. Anybody remember those old butcher shops with sawdust on the floor?

Mike pushed through a half-open door into a bedroom. He halted immediately and held out his hand for me to come no farther. I came anyway and pulled up alongside him.

I stared, saw what Mike had seen, and said softly, "Jeepers."

The man slumped with his back against the side of the bed was, without doubt, Nick Spitalny. We'd seen his mug shot in Captain Kingsley's office. He was heavy-set and big-bellied; squirrellike sideburns covered his fleshy jowls. He wore pajamas. They were soaked with blood in front. He was, in fact, sitting in a great big pool of blood which was now beginning to turn sticky.

"Don't touch anything, George," said Mike. "We now tiptoe out of here and make an anonymous phone call so the cops can find him."

"All that blood," I said, still staring, feeling a little sick.

"I know," said Mike. "It's something you never really get used to."

CHAPTER EIGHT

The murder of Nicholas M. Spitalny not only didn't make the headlines but, as far as I could determine, wasn't even mentioned in any major newspaper. It was just another homicide in greater Los Angeles that day; enough, if it had been given notice, to make a reader yawn and ask what else is new.

Mike and I thought we were home free after he, sounding like a flustered citizen, made his phone call to report the body and give the address. There was even a chance, it seemed, that Captain Kingsley wouldn't hear of the killing for a while. We congratulated ourselves on having pulled it off rather slickly. That, as we later discovered, was premature.

Shooting had been resumed by the time we returned to Chirapulco. With Phyllis Upton at the helm a more businesslike air had come over the set. People were showing up on time to a greater extent and trying harder to get the scenes wrapped up in as few takes as possible.

Joel Totterelli, with no one at his elbow telling him how to do his job, was directing in his own way and, understanding the need for saving time, giving up some of the utter, utter perfection he might have sought otherwise. He let it go and called it a take several times, for example, when Blossom Foster delivered her lines like a first-grader reciting Dick and Jane, because it would have taken hours to bring her to the point where she'd do it right by accident.

Once, after he'd accepted such a performance, we broke for lunch and I sat at an outdoor table with Joel. I said what maybe I shouldn't have said. Joel was the director, and I was just one of the actors. It was the great Alfred Hitchcock, I believe, who once observed that actors are cattle. But even a cow has to say moo once in a while.

"I don't know about that last scene," I said, frowning. "It might get a laugh. When there isn't supposed to be one."

"Blossom's tag line?" He sipped his scalding hot coffee with care. "Yeah, it was weak. But she's so overwhelmingly visual they might not pay much attention to the line. It'll have to stay in. I've got to finish at least five pages today. Not that I like it. But we'll never finish without rushing now. We're down to low-budget requirements, and we just have to face it."

"Maybe it won't be so bad," I said, trying to cheer myself up as much as him. "Maybe the rest of the picture—which really looks good—will carry these few scenes."

"Could be." Joel shrugged. "It scorches me, though. I don't have to tell you this film is a kind of comeback for me. They have to know I can stay off the sauce and direct as well as ever—maybe better than ever. Hell, *I* have to know it. First, I had to put up with Lance, though I must admit most of his ideas didn't ruin the picture; they just made it more expensive. Now I have to cut corners and turn out scenes I'm less than satisfied with." He sipped coffee again and showed a wry grin. "It's enough to drive a man back to drink."

I showed mock horror, which wasn't really so mock. "Not that, Joel. Of all things, not that."

"Don't worry. I've been reconditioned, thank God. The best thing that ever happened to me was getting steered to Alcoholics Anonymous. Their ideas really work. The main thing is acknowledging the problem—you have to admit it's there before you can deal with it. I wish to hell AA had a chapter here in Chirapulco. Corny as they are, I miss the meetings. They're all that keep you going sometimes."

* * *

That same evening Mike Corby and I dropped into Glenn Ford's room at the hotel to listen to Peter Revelstoke's bit on his shortwave set. He poured us some twelve-year-old scotch and we all sat back and relaxed, expecting nothing more than moderately useful industry gossip: what projects were on the fire, who was being hired for them, what execs were replacing each other in the continuing corporate game of musical chairs that goes on at all the networks and big studios, and all that sort of thing. Everybody in Hollywood hated Peter Revelstoke, but everybody listened to him. He seemed to know what was going on before many of the people involved did. Mike had theorized that he did it with a favorite police tool-of-the-trade—an excellent stable of informers.

Them we got in Hollywood. Rhona Barrett, when she had a network Hollywood-news shot, told me she got most of her scandal leads from the best friends of those who were being scandalized.

"The Godless," said Revelstoke, "now being shot on location, in Chirapulco, Mexico, is being plagued with so many sordid murders that someone has at last resorted to what amounts to a cover-up. Sir Walter Scott, in 'Lochinvar,' wrote the line that so aptly applies to what is going on. 'Oh, what a tangled web we weave, when first we practice to deceive!'"

"What the hell's he talking about?" I said, raising my head.

Mike waved at me. "Shhh!"

"I have it from a very reliable source," continued Revelstoke, "that a *certain* retired policeman, along with a *certain* prominent actor, both in the cast of this pedestrian horse opera, took it upon themselves to break into the home of a *certain* dealer in illicit arms while they attempted to investigate the unfortunate and still-mysterious death of producer Lance Haverford. In doing so, they violated the law. *Certain* officials of the Los Angeles Police Department know very well it was they who discovered the gun dealer's body after *he* had been shot to death by person or persons unknown. Or are they unknown? Was he, too, perhaps murdered by *certain* members of this meretricious movie? No information is being given out by police or anyone else on this incident and its possible connection with the other killings in Chirapulco."

"The bastard!" said Mike, staring at the radio.

The radio voice went on blithely. "The motion picture industry, which pervades the daily life of southern California, and has far reaching psychological influence on the rest of the country, has now become so powerful that its moral contamination, like that of the Mafia, reaches the highest levels of officialdom. . . ."

After he'd finished, we turned the radio off and stared at each other.

Looking at Mike, I said, "How the hell did he find out?"

"Who knows? That taxi driver for a guess. He knew who we were. Anyway, the cat's out of the bag."

"Are you two guys going to be in trouble?" asked Glenn.

Mike shook his head. "I don't think so. Though, technically, we probably could be slapped with a B and E. The real damage is to the picture, which already has an image that can't be sitting so well with J. Sutton Fargo and all his bible-thumping cronies."

"Look," I said, "we better let Phyllis know. She might want Ira to crank out a press release or something to counteract it."

Mike lit a cigarette and took a long sip of his scotch. "What bothers me now," he said, "is that maybe Nick Spitalny's death *is* connected with the others, as Revelstoke implies. For your information, Glenn, George and I did look up Spitalny. I figured a silencer was used on Lance and was trying to track it down. We didn't exactly bust into his house—the door was open. But we did find him dead; shot in the chest several times. My immediate reaction was that he'd been hit by somebody in what we loosely call the criminal world. A guy in Spitalny's business is bound to have enemies. I figured George and I just stumbled upon him at an unfortunate time."

"It was unfortunate, all right." I shuddered a little, remembering the sight of Spitalny's body.

"But now," continued Mike, "I'm thinking it's at least possible that whoever got that silencer from Spitalny—if he did—didn't want us to find out and wasted Spitalny to keep him from talking."

"If what you say is true," I said, frowning, "it means the killer knew we were trying to contact Spitalny. That would almost have to be somebody with the picture. Somebody who was in L.A. at the time we were. Even somebody who rode with us on the Citation!"

"Maybe." Mike was remaining calm and reflective. "First, anybody could have known what we were up to once Jenny Schwartz found out. Telling her anything's like taking a full-page ad in *Variety*. Second, we had a weekend and a three-day break. Anybody here in Chirapulco could have hopped into L.A. on one of the commercial flights without attracting much notice."

Glenn stared hard at Mike. "Look, Mike, I'm not a cop, though, like George, I've played a few in my time. All I know about solving crimes is from books or scripts I've read. But it seems to me that even a layman can play around with logic and make a few guesses."

"So, go ahead," said Mike, grinning.

"Well, why not take a good, hard look at those aboard the Citation with you, since they were closest to everything that happened? Consider them, at least as possible suspects, one by one?"

"Okay. A good, hard look. Where do you want to start?" Mike's dry smile said that he was challenging Glenn to come up with something that made sense, and he was fairly sure that Glenn wouldn't.

Glenn ticked off the names on his fingers as he mentioned them. "Passengers: Jennifer Schwartz, Roberta Vale, Ira Yoder, Phyllis Upton, Cora Foster, and Joel Totterelli. Pilots: Ferdy Holtz and George Kennedy. Just for the sake of argument, let's call them possible suspects, okay? And for the time being let's make another assumption. Let's assume that Trish Wainwright, Wally Demarest, Lance Haverford, and this Spitalny character were all killed by the same murderer. This is a tentative assumption, mind you, to allow us to explore our hypothesis."

"Go on," said Mike.

"Okay. Let's start with motive. Who, for some reason, would *want* to kill all these people? Was there an individual reason in each case or is it a kind of blanket motive? By that, I mean, is the murderer perhaps just killing off anyone who becomes vulnerable in order to create a series of murders that will damage the picture we're trying to shoot?"

"I don't know, and you don't know," said Mike. "At this point, nobody knows. You're speculating that somebody wants to ruin *The Godless*. Who, on that list of yours, would have any reason to?"

"Well," said Glenn, frowning, "that's part of the problem. As far as I can see, offhand, all those people would want *The Godless* to be a big success."

"Right," said Mike. "So maybe there is no motive, in the ordinary sense. Maybe the motive's all wrapped up in somebody's badly twisted mind. Something that makes sense to the killer, but is pointless to anybody else. This usually means no real connections with the victims and makes it very, very tough to zero in on the perpetrator. We almost have to catch the killer redhanded."

Glenn was nodding thoughtfully. "I see what you mean, Mike. But what you say gives me a rather somber thought."

"Yeah? What's that?"

"If some nut is roaming around here, picking off people by some kind of whim, then any one of us could be next!"

Mike sighed deeply. "Unfortunately," he said, "there's something in what you say...."

* * *

Although harried by the necessity of shooting too fast in order to catch up with the budget, Joel Totterelli was still striving to give his artistic best to the picture. He even fought to keep a scene Phyllis had planned to throw out because it called for extra setup time and wasn't too important plot-wise, or, at least, could be worked around by minor dialogue changes elsewhere.

It promised to be one hell of a scene. There was a strikingly beautiful spot in the gorge, a few miles down-stream from where Wally Demarest had fallen to his death. Here, the trickling stream met a natural dam of rocks and formed a delightful pool. Joel wanted to shoot Blossom Foster bathing in the nude there.

The scene wasn't in the original book and had been Lance Haverford's idea after the location scouts had dis-covered the pool. Lance, profligate as always, had brought the novelist, a grumpy old guy named Walt Sheldon, all the way down from Washington state to spend a week in Hollywood with the screen writers while they worked it into the plot. Joel had not only agreed with Lance but was himself in love with the idea.

I was there when Joel talked Phyllis into keeping the scene. He made a camera frame of his hands, thumbs together, and squinted through this as he outlined what he had in mind. No director can tell a story without this imaginary camera frame.

"It'll be one of these memorable scenes," said Joel, his usually placid eyes glowing with excitement for a change. "Here's Blossom in the pool—high-angle long-shot—and here's the young cowhand who's discovered her there—and we're looking at her from his P.O.V. He's too bashful to make his presence known, so he circles around, watching her. That's how the camera sees her, moving in these dreamy circles. He's falling in love with her in this moment, and so is the audience. She continues bathing and all her innocence is in it. The camera says how she feels and how he feels and foreshadows how, in a few moments, they'll be making love. When they do, we cut to the gurgling water, plunging downstream, on its eternal way from the mountains to the distant sea. Christ, even Peter Revelstoke will love it!"

"Well, I don't know," said Phyllis, frowning.

"A scene they'll talk about for years to come," Joel went on, overriding her. "Like Alan Ladd framed by the antlers of the deer as he approaches, riding, in *Shane*. Or Bogart walking off into the mist in *Casablanca*. At the very least, it'll make one hell of a publicity still, like that shot of Jane Russell in that off-the-shoulder blouse Howard Hughes used to promote *The Outlaw*."

"I don't know," Phyllis said again.

But her frown, which added creases to her wildebeest countenance, was softening.

"Maybe we can take something else out to make up for it," she finally said.

"We'll do that," said Joel. "I'll find something. I love you, Phyl."

"Go away with you," she said, almost blushing.

So the day finally came when the equipment was set up at the little pool in the rocks, and everyone who was needed was there, early in the morning, to begin the shooting. Although frontal nudity is no big deal these days, Cora Foster, Blossom's mother, insisted that she rehearse covered with something, and that spectators be barred during shooting, when she'd be nude. I was allowed because I was, in effect, Blossom's coach—though I could see that Cora didn't really like having me there.

As I stood, waiting—which is what ninety percent of the people involved in a motion picture are doing ninety percent of the time—I had a random thought of which I was somewhat ashamed the moment I put it together. Mike Corby had suggested looking for a weird psychological motive behind the murders, and it came to me abruptly that excessive prudery can be psychologically weird—a symptom of deeper, darker twists in someone's mind. Was Cora Foster, of all people, getting even with assorted persons who, in her mind, had exposed her precious daughter to too much immorality?

I shook my head. Absurd. In fact, if anybody were

96

suspect on the grounds of fierce morality, it would be J. Sutton Fargo, who apparently equated a casual roll in the hay, anywhere, with the decline and fall of the United States of America.

I mention all these thoughts not for what they were worth—which wasn't much—but to show you how the apparent murders were dominating all our thoughts even when we were concentrating on other matters.

So I stood near Joel, behind the camera, and watched. The first shot was from high on the bank, looking down into the pool. The shiny boards were all set up to reflect light upon Blossom, and the director of photography had taken his meter readings and distance measurements, and Blossom was standing in the pool, while the young cow-hand was ready on the opposite bank to walk into the shot when Joel cued him.

"Rolling," said the camera operator.

"Quiet everybody!" called Jennifer, pressing her clipboard tightly to her mammoth breast.

Joel nodded to the assistant with the clap-boards. He stepped in front of the camera and smacked them. In case you're not familiar with the procedure, it works like this: what's written on the clap-board slate identifies the scene and take, and when the boards bang together they make a peak on the sound track so that the editor can match everything later from a single starting point.

"Speed!" called the sound man, squatting at his equipment.

"Action!" said Joel.

Blossom began to splash herself with water from the pool, which she scooped up in her cupped hands. If she couldn't deliver dialogue too well, she could at least move gracefully, and, as Joel wanted, she was making a kind of ballet out of it. It looked very good. I was sure it would be a wrap, the very first try. With Lance that would have been unheard of. He would have shot it several times and then, like as not, gone back to the first take.

The alien sound that then intruded into the scene did

so insidiously, with a moment or two in the beginning during which we were not sure there was a sound. But suddenly we all heard the growling of an engine as some kind of vehicle, coming down the donkey trail, approached our location.

"Oh, Christ!" said Joel. "Cut! Cut!"

Everybody stopped whatever he or she was doing and turned to look.

A jeep joggled toward us over the bumps and ruts. It was filled with khaki-clad Mexican policemen, some of whom sat on the fender platforms, and all of whom held rifles. In the back seat, wearing a wild-looking flowered sports shirt in great contrast to the others, was tall and bulky Alfonso Cruz.

The jeep stopped, Cruz got out, and the policemen got out and deployed themselves around him. He scanned all of our astonished faces, then said, "Who is in charge here?"

"I guess that's me," said Joel, stepping forward.

"Ah," said Cruz. "Senor Totterelli, the director, I believe. Is Senor Mike Corby here?"

"No. He's not in this scene."

"Ah," said Cruz again. I thought he looked disappointed. "But everyone here—" He made a general wave with his hand. "They are involved in what you are doing, no?"

"Of course. What's this all about?"

Cruz took a big breath, in and out, shifted his legs to plant himself more firmly in the dust, and said, "It is with regret, senor, that I must inform you that you are in violation of Ordinance 384-12, sections B and C, of the city of Chirapulco."

"Huh?" said Joel.

"It has to do with committing, or encouraging to be committed, lewd and lascivious behavior within the limits of our jurisdiction, which extend out here, similar to your county divisions in the United States."

"I'm sorry," said Joel, looking puzzled. "That sounds like double-talk to me."

"I assure you it is not. How can I put this more plainly?" He nodded toward the gorge, where Blossom had already come ashore, and where Cora had rushed forward to wrap her in a big towel. "We have a law against indecent exposure. There have been complaints. I am forced to take action."

A canny expression came over Joel's clean-cut features. "I take it that with the proper contribution to some, uh, worthy cause this matter can be adjusted?"

After a long pause, during which his ripe-olive eyes smoldered quietly, Cruz said, "Not this time, senor. I know you Americans think a bribe can fix anything in the Republic of Mexico, and sometimes, I must confess, it can. But not this time."

"Now, wait a minute. You mean to say you're making a big deal out of this?"

"Yes. That is what it is. A big deal. I must ask you all—everyone here—to come with me."

"Where to?"

"*El jusgado*," said Cruz. "Or, in your American pronunciation, the hoosegow. . . ."

The huge cage in the Chirapulco police station was everything you wanted to know but were afraid to find out, first hand, about a Mexican jail. It was in the center of the building and rose two stories high to where the second-floor office rooms were laid along a kind of mezzanine or balcony. It reminded me of a bird cage at a zoo, built for a number of species to fly in.

It stank. The odor was a blend of soap and shit, though as far as I could see neither was on hand. I don't know how the policemen who worked all day in the headquarters were able to bear that odor.

From a security standpoint, there was a certain efficiency to it. All the cops around could look into the cage at all times and see what we were doing; there was no real need for guards. It was empty when we arrived, and I didn't know whether its previous occupants had been removed or whether we'd just hit it on a day when business was slow.

There were benches inside the cage on which about half of us could sit at any given time, and anyone who wanted to go to the toilet could signal for someone's attention and be escorted there. The cops all around us looked at us often, usually grinning. I don't think any of them were ready to inflict physical harm upon us, but they were clearly enjoying our humiliation.

Alfonso Cruz, in his second-floor office, was seeing us privately, one by one. When my turn came, I marched up there between two villainous-looking policemen who kept their hands near their revolvers.

"Ah, Mr. Kennedy!" said Cruz, as I entered. "Please come in. Please sit down."

I took a wooden chair across the desk from him. He sat there, half-smiling, until the silence got so long-drawn-out I was compelled to break it. I think that was what he wanted: for me to speak first and thus be on the psychological defensive.

"How long are you gonna hold us here, anyway?"

"That depends, senor. There is, of course, a great deal of paperwork and you will necessarily be detained at least until that is finished. Sometime tomorrow, I would estimate. What happens after that is up to the magistrate. There is a possibility that you may be held for trial."

"Don't we get a chance to call in a lawyer or something?"

"Of course. But that also takes a little time. We must proceed step by step."

"Captain," I said, frowning, "I find this all hard to believe. All the trouble and expense you've gone to in order to enforce some obscure local blue law—"

He held up his palm to interrupt me. "Not obscure, senor. Many of our citizens are god-fearing and take the protection of public morals quite seriously. But you are correct in suspecting that I have more than stamping out vice in mind."

"Okay, what *do* you have in mind?"

He leaned back and made a little steeple of his fingers on the rolling landscape of his tummy. "I was a little surprised that Senor Corby was not among those of you I arrested today. If I had him in jail it would serve as a warning. I asked him quite courteously, you know, to refrain from investigating the murders, but apparently this was not enough."

"You mean you hauled us all in here just to get Mike out of the way? Doesn't that come under the heading of overkill?"

Cruz shrugged. "The arrests have a certain value in improving my position with our citizens. We policemen need good will with the public, just as policemen in your country do. But they also serve to demonstrate that I am quite serious in my request to Senor Corby. He seems to be a close friend of yours, Mr. Kennedy. Perhaps you are the one to talk to him and even persuade him to desist. I do not think he will want his colleagues to be sitting in my jail any longer than necessary."

"I think I get it," I said. "Mike promises to lay off, and we get released, is that it?"

"I did not say that, senor. I could not say a thing like that officially. Besides, even I can't effect your release immediately now that the arrest has been made. The procedures that have already begun must be completed." He reached for his cigarettes. "Of course, I *could* speed matters a bit if I felt I would no longer have to put up with interference in my other investigations—"

"I'll pass that along to Mike," I said. "Do I get to see him? Do any of us get to see anybody?"

"During proper visiting hours, yes," Cruz said smugly. "We must observe regulations."

There is no greater observer of regulations than a Mexican bureaucrat. There are so many that he can usually find those he wishes to observe. This always takes time. Sometimes they complain that Mexico's a poor country, but if time is money they've got more of it than anybody else. While we all languished in the jail—taking turns sleeping on the benches that night—other members of the company who had finally heard about the mass arrest descended upon police headquarters and went through frantic motions to try to get us released. Phyllis Upton, as I learned later, having discovered that bribery wouldn't take care of it this time, got on the horn to L.A. and called the company's lawyers, making them promise to fly here as soon as possible, dropping all the multi-million-dollar corporate suits they were working on. They hemmed and hawed and said they would have to dig up an expert on Mexican law to bring with them, and also that they would have to retain an attorney of record in the town itself, and they made ten or twenty other objections, but all Phyllis would say was, "Do it, goddamnit! Whatever it costs!"

Cost it would. Lance, who always bought the best, had retained a law firm whose fees made F. Lee Bailey's look like pocket change.

I didn't get to see Mike Corby until after breakfast the next morning. The breakfast I won't mention because I couldn't eat most of it and don't want the memory of even what little I tasted. I was brought to a visiting room where Mike sat across a table from me, while a guard who looked like he should have been one of the *bandidos* instead of one of the cops stood at the door and kept a sour eye upon us.

"Where the hell have you been?" I asked Mike.

"Well, Meredy and I slipped off for a picnic. We went to a little town where they've got all this scenery she was sketching. You know, I think she must be a pretty good artist. Anyway, we didn't get back till late yesterday, and then we heard how you'd all been arrested."

"Okay," I said, "if you can take enough time off from your love life, I've got a message for you. From Cruz. Maybe he'll tell you the same thing in person when he sees you, but I think he wants me to pass it along too, for emphasis. The message—as I understand it—is that he wants you to lay off the murder investigation. Otherwise we all rot in jail for God knows how long."

Mike nodded. "I've already got that little message. I figured that was it the moment I knew you'd all been picked up. I wouldn't have thought it likely, but it seems Cruz has a way of finding out what I'm up to, even when I'm in L.A."

"In that case, why not go along with him? Forget all this professional pride—if that's what it is—and drop the investigation."

"Well," said Mike, his frown deepening, "it's starting to get just a little too hot for that now."

"What do you mean, too hot?"

"I checked some of those weekend departures by commercial flight when we took the Citation to L.A. Meredy got the names at the airport. Her Spanish is better than mine. What this all boils down to is that another six persons—I can't exactly call them suspects—in addition to those Ferdy flew back—were in L.A. when Spitalny was iced. Guess who they were."

"I don't want to guess who they were, goddamnit! You tell me."

"Okay, okay," said Mike, calming me down and making me realize how touchy the hours in the Mexican jailhouse had made me. "From the cast and crew, Dean Martin and Raquel Welch—"

"Couldn't be either of them."

Mike shrugged. "You can say that about any of the suspects. Let me finish the list. Sam Rubicoff, the stunt coordinator."

"Sam? I've known him for a long time."

"Stop interrupting. The other three aren't connected with the picture. But, in one way or another, they're all sort of connected with the murders. First, Senor Mendoza y Villasenor, or Ernie, as Trish called him. Apparently he flies to L.A. all the time, probably to pick up thousand-dollar trinkets for his various girlfriends on Rodeo Drive. If that makes me sound gossipy, like Jennifer Schwartz, sorry. It's what a murder investigation sometimes leads to."

"Come on, Mike," I said. "Who else?"

"Okay, next is Luis Mondragon, better known as 'The Scorpion,' killer of bulls and Wally Demarest's former boyfriend. It's unusual for either a stunt man or a matador to be gay, and when you're looking into a murder you have to consider whatever is unusual. So Luis is going to require further thought."

I ticked off names on my fingers. "Dean, Raquel, Sam Rubicoff, Ernie Mendoza, and Luis. That's five. Who's our last wayward traveler?"

"I've been saving him," said Mike, grinning. "None other than Captain of Detectives Alfonso Cruz!"

"What?"

"I know," said Mike. "I guess he had business with LAPD. Maybe he was checking up on *me*, and the way I got that poison analyzed. Anyway, I know how you feel. How could *he* be a suspect? Would he commit a bunch of murders just so he could solve them and get transferred out of the boondocks? That's a crazy idea, but no crazier than most ideas I've had lately."

I sighed. "Mike, how about dropping the investigation long enough to concentrate on getting us out of here?"

"I'll try," he said. "But I don't know if I'll have much success with that project either. . . ."

CHAPTER NINE

I wasn't exactly the Bird Man of Alcatraz, but four days in that miserable jail were enough to make me feel I'd spent a lifetime behind bars, and the outside world seemed like an alien environment once I encountered it again.

We were released without ceremony, but not without procedure, as we stood in line to sign things and receive our personal effects before walking out into the brilliant sunshine. That night we celebrated in the hotel cantina. The way things were, it was closer to a wake than a celebration.

The lawyers who flew down from L.A. had spent their days in frantic maneuvering and their nights getting smashed on mescal and tequila in the cantina. Through the local *abogado*, who did the actual representation as our attorney, they finally arrived at an agreement that the morals charge would be dropped if the company would, instead, pay a whopping fine for trespassing—on whose land I never did find out.

In the cantina, I sat with Mike and Meredy, and with one of the lawyers—a big, bearded guy named Aloysius Cuddyback. His name wasn't the only improbable thing about him.

Instead of a corporate lawyer's dark suit, Cuddyback wore blue jeans and a Three Musketeers shirt open at the chest to show his curly hair and a necklace of multicolored love beads. He had a gold ring in one ear. He belted down the mescal as though it were Seven-Up.

"Like, I used to be in criminal law," he said, "but that's not where the bread is. I mean, courtroom drama and all that shit, but who can pay the bills on it?"

"If it's that cheap," said Mike, "how about some free advice?"

"I'm not drunk enough yet to give out any free advice," said Cuddyback. "And when I am, the advice is no good."

"We'll take it anyway," said Mike. He turned to Meredy. I'd met her for the first time this evening, and liked her immediately. She was open and fresh and smiled readily and took everything in stride. She also endeared herself to me, ham that I am at heart, by recalling many of my motion-picture roles and knowing what was good about them. I'm sure she knew what was bad, too, but she didn't bring that up. Mike said to her, "Tell him, huh?"

"Tell him what?"

"Your long, sad tale. How you jumped bail and how every bounty hunter in the West is looking for you."

"Oh, that," said Meredy. "It's hardly worth telling."

Then she proceeded to tell it, and Cuddyback's eyes warmed up with interest as he listened and interjected questions to clarify certain points. Like Mike, the lawyer was apparently unable to resist a professional challenge.

"Basically," he said to Meredy, "and if everything is like you said, the rap can be beat. The time that's passed, the probable disinterest of the prosecution, and the fact that they don't want the expense of running it through court again, would be in your favor. You could come out of it with as little as a suspended sentence and probation. It would take a good lawyer to do it, preferably one who's on the scene and used to making deals with the prosecution on a buddy-buddy first-name basis, and you'd be better off with somebody real sharp—like me— behind the scenes, calling the shots. It would cost money."

"I was afraid of that," said Mike.

"Everybody is," said Cuddyback, shrugging. "I don't know why I drink this goddamned mescal. It tastes like gasoline...."

As Mike and Meredy continued discussing her case with the lawyer—by some strange chemistry the three of them got along marvelously—I wandered over to the bar where I saw Phyllis Upton sitting alone. She was glumly drinking a tall iced drink.

"You looked lonely sitting here, miss," I said, "and I thought I'd introduce myself. My name is George H. Kennedy. Haven't we met somewhere before?"

"Why, sir!" she said, smiling, picking it up. "I am not used to being accosted by perfect strangers!"

I took a stool next to her. "Don't worry, I'm not perfect. Buy you a drink?"

"Thanks. I'm having trouble finishing this one." She sighed. "That's the hell of it. I really don't get accosted."

"That's good. Saves a lot of aggravation."

"Which I'd be willing to put up with. Know what my big trouble is, George? That I'm a woman."

"That's trouble?"

"With me, it is. If I were a man—or even a lesbian—I could look the way I do and nobody would bat an eye. It's unfair."

"Look, Phyl," I said, "I don't want to go into a lot of clichés about beauty being skin deep, etcetera, but you have got a lot of qualities anybody with any taste might well admire."

"I'd give them all up for bitchy good looks," she said, staring at nothing. "I get lonely."

"We all do. At times." This was a challenge for me now; I wanted to make her feel better.

"Know something?" Phyllis was apparently in a mood to let her hair down. (It was all wrong, by the way, the way it was coiffed. Same with her sleeveless shirt and boldly checked slacks, which accentuated her bowling-pin figure.) "I tried everybody from a cosmetician to a shrink and not one of them did me any good. I even went to a plastic surgeon, and all he did was make excuses about having a full schedule."

"Forget it," I said. "We've been rescued from durance vile and this is a time for celebration."

"It's not, really," she said. She turned her toadlike eyes upon me. "George, we are up to our ass in alligators."

"We are?"

"Do you have any idea what this four-day delay and all these lawyers have cost us?"

"Plenty, I'm sure."

"To say nothing of cutting Blossom's nude scene short. Of course, the sound man picked up room tone, so some of it could be salvaged, but there wasn't as much as Joel wanted so he could really have enough angles to choose from and make it a masterpiece."

"Where is Joel, anyway?"

"Somewhere sulking, I imagine," said Phyllis, with a shrug.

"Phyl," I said earnestly, "on the finances—are we really going to make it?"

"Not with what's earmarked," she said, shaking her head. "We might finish the location shooting—just barely. But I don't have to tell you what we need for postproduction. Titles, music, opticals, retakes, and everything, as usual, twice as expensive as you thought it would be. If Fargo or somebody doesn't come through with a little more, we're sunk. In the old days we'd have been able to find backing somewhere else—at the very least somebody to buy what we've already got and finish it."

I didn't mean to, but somehow I said the wrong thing. It slipped out before I could think. "If Lance were still here," I said, "he'd work another one of his miracles and find some backing somewhere."

It wasn't meant as a criticism of Phyllis, but that must have been how she took it. Her eyes flared, the way a fire comes up when you sprinkle a few drops of gasoline on it. "Lance ran out of miracles when he got that bullet in his head!" she said.

Anything else I said would have made it worse, so I dropped that subject and didn't bring it up again.

The hotel rooms were all reached by outer balconies which, in turn, were accessible by outside stairs, and long before the moon was too high that night most mem-

108

bers of the company drifted out of the cantina to seek a good night's sleep in real beds—especially those who hadn't enjoyed that luxury in the jail. The lawyers, who were flying out the next morning, plus a few diehard celebrants, stayed on and kept the mescal flowing, but the majority had Phyllis's call sheet for an early hour in mind and were, indeed, anxious to get to work and start the shooting rolling again.

Both Mike and I were on call, for a later scene Joel might or might not get to; we could look forward to most of a whole day standing around in costume and just waiting. I told Mike I was thinking of borrowing a golf club from Dean Martin and learning to hit horse turds with it. He said that sounded like as good a sport as any and might catch on.

Meredy insisted on taking herself home so Mike could get the sleep he needed, and kissed everybody goodnight, including the bearded lawyer in the blue jeans. Mike and I found the stairs in back that led to our rooms.

"Nice gal," I said to Mike.

"Yeah," he said.

By that exchange I knew that a serious romance was probably in the works.

"It's gotta be clear sailing from now on," I said. The smell of night blooms was sweet and delicate here where the garden wrapped itself around the rear of the hotel. "I don't see what else can happen. We've had our share." I looked heavenward for a moment. "Haven't we?"

"You'd think so," said Mike. We started up the stairs. "I could be making phone calls tomorrow. Getting more dope on all the people who were in L.A. when Spitalny got iced. I wonder if Joel really needs me."

I shrugged. "Ask him."

Joel Totterelli's room was on the second level and we had to pass it to get to our own rooms. As we approached it, I saw that the door was partly open and that there was a light inside. It was my guess Joel was still going over the script, trying to figure where he could cut

109

corners and finish an unheard-of number of pages the next day.

I had already decided that if anybody could finish up *The Godless* under the handicap of being pressed for time, it was Joel. He'd started his career as a mail-room clerk in a major studio, moved up from that to production assistant, and then, through a series of chores that were all apprenticeships, had become a film editor—an immensely important job the public never gives enough credit to. He finally got to direct a cheapie horror film that, in spite of its absurd plot about a guy who grew two heads, attracted notice because it was done so very well. After that, he directed other pictures and eventually, as you probably know, won an Oscar for *Such Stuff as Dreams*.

Joel had the reputation of always being calm, always agreeable, always in control. The most temperamental of stars were delighted to work with him, and he knew how to handle them. He could rebuke them and make them think they'd just received an accolade. But when he started to hit the sauce he really changed. It was Jekyll and Hyde all over again. He wouldn't show up, or he would screw everything up when he did, and before long everybody knew he was poison in the industry. He ended up in a drying-out farm for the requisite twenty-eight days and in time Alcoholics Anonymous got hold of him. He was selling real estate in the Silver Lake area when Lance Haverford found him and asked him to direct *The Godless*. Only Lance, a mad gambler at heart, would have taken the chance. Part of being a genius is being lucky.

Mike knocked on the partly opened door. There was no answer. "Hey—you in there, Joel?" called Mike. There was still no answer.

So Mike pushed open the door. The room was empty. The light in it came from a couple of table lamps that had been left on.

Ordinarily, Mike would have closed the door again, and we would have continued on our way. But at that point Mike and I—both at the same time—spotted the empty pint bottle of vodka and the empty glass on the coffee table beside an opened script and a number of other scattered papers.

"What the hell," said Mike. He stalked inside and I followed in his wake.

Joel was neither in the bathroom nor under the bed, though Mike looked in both places. I frowned at the vodka bottle. "Could have been someone else in here with him."

"Maybe," said Mike. I could see by his scowl that he didn't believe it. He leaned over the papers on the coffee table and started to read them, shuffling them aside, one by one. They'd been torn from a legal-size yellow pad Joel had evidently used to make notes upon. The notes, mostly in Joel's own abbreviations, which amounted to a code, had to do with his plans for blocking out the next day's scenes. Mike lifted one sheet that had a single note, scrawled in large, somewhat shaky hand-writing so that not all of it was quite legible. He squinted at it several ways and finally read, "Meet at set. 2 A.M. Take jeep."

"So?" I asked, wondering why he'd singled out this one.

"Look at the handwriting," he said, shoving the note at me. "Not like when he's sober. He must have been bombed. He must have written it tonight. He must have fallen off the wagon tonight."

I groaned. "We were wondering what else could happen. This could be what else."

"We better find him."

"The cantina in town, maybe?"

Mike looked at his watch. "Not one-thirty yet. He could have gone out to the set, like the note says. He could have left just minutes ago."

"'Meet at set,'" I said, rereading the note. "I wonder who he was supposed to meet?"

"What difference does it make? Come on, George,

let's get him and try to sober him up before it becomes absolutely impossible."

The company's vehicles were parked in various places—wherever there was space—around the hotel. Those of us above a certain level on the totem pole had keys to some of the cars in case we wanted to use them outside of working hours. My key was to a nondescript and undistinguished five-year-old Chevy sedan, and, never having used it, I'd almost forgotten I carried the key. Mike and I found the beast, climbed into it, and took off. The moon was now the color of fat on prime roast beef and it provided considerable illumination. I don't know if you've ever noticed—as a matter of fact, you're not supposed to notice—but in many motion pictures, night scenes are shot in the daytime through a filter that gives the effect of night. Technically, this is called "day-for-night" shooting; it always looks a little phony. That was what the dusty, rolling landscape just outside of town looked like now—a little phony. But it was real enough, and so was the crisis we had on our hands.

The road was paved for a short distance beyond the city limits, but with all the potholes in it, and warped slabs of concrete, it might as well not have been. I held the sedan somewhere between fifty and sixty and fought with the wheel as I tried to anticipate the bumps. Several times we seemed to skid on two wheels around the un-banked turns. I definitely had to slow up for the sharp turn into the unpaved road that led to the set.

"Jeepers," I said, employing, like the cowboys of old, my favorite private cussword, "we ought to have Paul Newman driving this thing. He races, you know."

"I know," growled Mike. "Keep driving."

Moments after that, we picked up a pair of red tail-lights ahead. As we gained upon them slowly, we saw that they were swishing from side to side.

"That's gotta be Joel," I said. "It's nobody sober, anyway."

"Why the hell did he have to fall off the wagon now? Seems to me he wasn't having all that much pressure."

"It was pressure to *him*—whatever was bugging him. I think I read somewhere that alcoholics tend to be intelligent and very sensitive. Always in delicate balance."

"Maybe," said Mike. "But Joel had it licked. What I'm really wondering is—did somebody *push* him off the wagon?"

"Why would they?"

"I don't know. For the same reason somebody's committing murders? To hurt the picture?"

"But who wants to hurt the picture? Everybody's got a stake in it."

"Can you go faster, George?"

"Goddamnit," I said, "I'm trying."

Slowly . . . agonizingly . . . we narrowed the gap between us and the car ahead. We could see now that it was, indeed, one of the jeeps. The slim silhouette of the person driving it seemed to be Joel. As far as we could tell, he hadn't looked back yet, though his rear-view mirror could have told him he was being followed. At any rate, he wasn't slowing up, and his vehicle was still swaying, sometimes hitting the soft shoulder on either side of the road.

Although neither of us had said so, we both feared that at any moment the jeep ahead might go off the road, which could be either good or bad. At best, it would bog down in the softer earth and come to a halt. At worst, it would overturn. A highway patrolman had once told me that drunks tend to drive too slowly rather than too fast, and that was how he often spotted them. Joel, ahead— if it was Joel—was being an exception to that rule.

And then it happened.

What happened was not precisely what we'd expected, although everything came so fast we didn't have time to examine that realization. First, there was an explosion—an eruption of orange flame that made a big ball, five or six feet high, just above the jeep. We saw it and, an instant later, heard the thudding sound of it. The jeep careened, obviously out of control, and went off the side of the road, where it took a full turn, virtually in mid-air, and then crashed on its side. We saw the body fly from it and hit the desert scree a few feet away from it.

I braked the sedan to a jolting stop and we piled out of it. We ran to the body. It was Joel.

He was on his back and in a twisted position. His eyes were wide open and still as they looked upward toward all the crushed-ice stars sprinkled on the Mexican night.

CHAPTER TEN

When the shock of someone's death hits you, all that follows immediately becomes a blur in your memory; you know you did this and that, and you know you went from here to there, but the precise steps are unclear. Real life becomes like a motion picture in which you cut from one scene to the next, and to hell with what happened between. But what happened in the few dark hours after Mike and I had witnessed Joel's accident had a bearing on all that followed and was too important to be forgotten entirely.

The first decision that Mike made was that he would stay at the scene while I drove back to town to notify the police. He put this in the form of a suggestion, but it was actually a command. He was in charge, and I tacitly acknowledged that. Sudden death, after all, was his bag.

"We want to be sure nothing's disturbed," he explained. "I don't know who'd disturb it, but you never can tell."

"It's okay, Mike," I said. "I can see it's the best way."

"Right. And I suppose you're thinking what I am. This may not have been just an accident."

I nodded. "That's exactly what I'm thinking. The explosion just before he went off the road—"

"Yeah. Did it strike you as familiar?"

"Familiar? No. I've never seen anything like this before."

"I think you have," said Mike, his eyes thoughtful. "Crash scenes . . . special effects. . . ."

"Oh, that." Now my eyes became thoughtful. "Like,

115

when they put a time charge in so the car will explode when they want it to. Of course. It *did* look like that."

"Suppose," continued Mike, "somebody stuck a charge in the jeep. Maybe knowing Joel would get himself sauced up and then try to drive it. Maybe setting it up—asking Joel to meet somebody at the set, like the note said. The charge might not be enough to kill him for sure, but it would be enough to make him crash, which probably would kill him. Anyway, the whole thing would look like an accident."

"But why make some of these killings look like accidents, and others look like what they are—killings?"

"I don't know. But it may be to our advantage this time to keep this looking like an accident. Until we can prove otherwise. So when you report this to the cops— especially if you get to talk to Cruz—kind of forget that first explosion, okay?"

"Forget it? Why?"

"God knows what Cruz'll do if he thinks it's murder again. He may stick everybody back in the bucket, on the excuse that we're all suspects. Or he may get disgusted and have us all sent home. Then the picture really would never get finished."

I tried to untangle this in my head. "You mean—if this is murder—we just let the murderer get away with it?"

"For the moment," said Mike, nodding. "I'll look into it, of course, and if I find anything I'll let Cruz know. But not until we finish shooting here on location. Hell, we can't have more than a couple of weeks left."

"If Phyl decides to continue without Joel," I said.

"She's got to," said Mike. "No other choice."

I nodded slowly, then turned and walked back to our sedan to drive it into town.

Mike's strategy of letting Joel's death appear to be an accident worked to a degree—at least Captain of Detectives Alfonso Cruz made no immediate moves to get us all deported. But he couldn't have been entirely mollified. He must have wondered about the incident, as everyone else did.

Most of the next day was taken up by all the activity a violent death generates—statements had to be recorded, scores of people had to be notified, the body had to be removed and arrangements made to ship it home, and what all this amounted to was no shooting—everything cancelled and another twenty-four hour delay.

I began to suspect that we were lucky in enduring only this much delay. The whole project was very close to coming to a halt—not so much a grinding halt as a sudden flop, flat on its face. Everybody was uncomfortable and some were ready to walk off the picture, or at least talk Phyllis into cancelling all the shooting so that they'd be fired and no longer saddled by contractual obligations, to say nothing of the bad reputation one gets when he leaves on his own.

Even Dean Martin—a trouper in the old-fashioned show-must-go-on sense—had reservations about continuing. I had coffee with him at a late breakfast at the hotel, and, with a most uncomfortable frown he said, "You know what I think Phyllis ought to do? Fold here, on location, as of right now. Go back to Hollywood and somehow shoot around all the existing footage to get some kind of a finished product."

Mariette Hartley, who had joined us at the table, frowned and nodded. "If there's anything I don't like it's being temperamental," she said. I nodded. Mariette's marvelously easy to work with—never a problem to anyone. "But—" She paused—

"Let me finish it for you. The way things are you just can't get all these murders and accidents out of your mind. You can't concentrate on your job."

"That's about it," said Mariette. "I'm glad you said it for me."

"Not only for you—for most of us," I said. "Those who aren't distracted are scared to death they might be next. And I don't blame them."

I didn't have to talk to the other members of the cast

117

and crew to know that they all felt as uncomfortable, as restless, as mixed-up as Dean and Mariette. I didn't need an explanation. It was in the air—like the stink of a dead rat buried in a wall somewhere.

But, as I suspected, Phyllis wasn't about to declare any holidays. And she had a surprise for me. I didn't foresee it and, at first, wondered why she left a message for me to meet her in her administrative trailer out on the set. When I walked in I saw her behind her desk scribbling in a ledgerlike book she had spread open in front of her. She continued writing whatever it was as I came in—looking up, smiling (even her smile failed to brighten her warthog features a great deal, poor gal) and saying, "I'll be with you in a second, George. This is a running journal I keep of everything that happens. Makes a handy reference later."

"I see," I said. I wasn't really listening and was still wondering why she'd called me.

"Now," said Phyllis, closing the journal. "There has to be a director with Joel gone. How about you?"

"Me?"

"You always wanted to direct, didn't you? I know you've been in this business long enough to know all the things a director must know, and I know you've made yourself ready for it. If I call somebody else in, that means another delay—and more expense. So how about taking over?"

"You know I will," I answered. "But to be honest with you, Phyllis, I can't give you any guarantees. Just that I'll do my damndest."

"I know that, George. I'll be honest with you, too. The few scenes we have left—and that you'll direct—perhaps won't have the exquisite touches Lance or Joel might have put into them. But at the very least you'll give me—I'm sure—a good, workmanlike job, and at least the picture will get finished. Right now, that's the name of the game. Unless something else happens." She sighed deeply. "Are we really jinxed? Is there really such a thing?"

"If there is," I said, "we can't afford to believe in it."

This was the obvious reaction everywhere, of course. *The Godless* was jinxed. It was not only Peter Revelstoke who dwelled on that supposition now. Everybody in the media, even the nice guys and gals, took up the cry, which, after all, made good copy. It spilled out of the slop bucket of gossip and into the regular news. *Time*, *Newsweek*, and *TV Guide* all carried pieces on it, and it made the CBS Evening News, along with some footage of activity on the set that Ira Yoder most reluctantly supplied. He didn't want them to do the story, but he had to keep them happy.

For the first time I encountered what I suppose every director has to learn to put up with—how to deal with a temperamental star. In this case, the star was Alex Keglmeyer, whose name should be immediately recognizable to those of you under thirty (and I might add that you constitute a very large portion of our box-office clientele, so God bless you all). Alex, a young multimillionaire, was very big in the rock-music field before he was chosen to play the part of Joe, the young half-breed cowhand—the same one who had the pool scene with Blossom Foster—in *The Godless*. This was his first acting effort and in the tests he had looked quite good. A Eurasian, Alex had been born in Japan, where his father, serving in the U.S. military, had married a lovely daughter of Nippon, and he was physically perfect for the part. He had an offbeat handsomeness that I thought might someday take him all the way, if he'd add enough humility to it to learn his craft.

Frowning, he took me aside in the hotel cantina and with much hemming and hawing spoke his piece.

"Like, you know, George, what's hangin' on us here, is, you know, totally groady."

As the father of a small army of teen-age daughters, I understood his mode of speech, which was closely related to Valley Language, used by many young persons

119

in the San Fernando Valley, though not nearly as much as some of the life-style reporters would have you believe.

"It is, huh?" I said.

"So what I mean is, you know, it frosts my gord to do this, but I think I gotta, like, walk off the set. Drop it with a bang, you know what I mean?"

"Walk off? You can't do that!"

He fidgeted. "I checked with my agent by phone. Like, he thinks I could wriggle out of it, contract-wise. Anyway, getting sued is better than getting killed."

"What do you mean, getting killed!" I stared at him in disbelief.

"This damn picture has a squeege on it—a jinx—just like they say. How do I know I won't be the next one to get it?"

My stare turned into a glare. "You walk off and it'll get around. Your name will be mud. You may never make another picture—maybe never even another commercial."

He shrugged. "So, like I go back to blowing guitar."

"And how long does that last? The record business is way down, like everything else. I even hear there's a trend back to Lawrence Welk."

"Totally repulsive!" he said. "Anything but that!"

"Goddamnit," I said, "you made it by looking macho—getting up there with your shirt off and showing your muscles while you wiggled and sang—mostly wiggled. Is that a completely phony image? Under all those muscles are you nothing but a scared little kid?"

"You got no right to say that, George!"

"I've got every right! I don't want to see this picture blown, and I don't want to see you, with your potential as an actor, blown!"

He frowned. "Well, I guess maybe I do have, like, some pretty good possibilities—"

"This is your big chance, Alex," I said, my voice taking on a softer tone. "The big chances only come along once or twice in your whole life. I know. I've been there. If you don't grab the brass ring now you never will."

"Well . . . maybe." His frown deepened.

"And look at the publicity Ira could whip up for you. 'Rock Star Sticks in Spite of Danger.' Those pissy teenage fans of yours will love you more than ever. They'll have orgasms in their tight jeans at the very mention of your name!"

"I suppose you gotta think about the fans," he said, still frowning, but now nodding.

"I'll see you on the set tomorrow," I said. "Bright and early."

I still don't know whether he was serious, or whether he just wanted his ego stroked. Anyway, I handled it and figured I was learning a few things I hadn't anticipated about the art of directing.

I've heard all sorts of theories about what distinguishes man from other animals, but one of the things I've noticed personally is that he, and apparently he alone, complains. When I was an actor I bitched about all the time on my hands. Now that I was a director I grumbled because I never had enough time. But I tried to keep the complaints to myself, or aired them only to those very close to me, like Mike Corby.

Of whom I was seeing very little. I knew that he was continuing his investigation of the murders, taking care to conceal that from Alfonso Cruz, but, touching base with Mike only occasionally, I had no idea what progress he was making. If any.

The first chance I had to discuss the matter at length with Mike came the evening he brought some of Meredy's paintings to the hotel lobby, where he and Meredy, with the help of some of the hotel staff, proceeded to hang them.

The exhibition had been Mike's idea. As he admitted, he didn't know how good her paintings were, but it occurred to him that some of the members of the company might like to buy a few. The prices were right—probably

121

even too low—and there were bound to be art lovers among us. It was too bad Vincent Price wasn't in this movie; he buys paintings the way you and I buy sticks of gum, and he knows whether they're good or bad. Anyway, if the exhibition brought Meredy some extra cash, she could use it. She'd decided to save up for some of that expensive legal help she'd need when she could bring herself to recross the border and pick up where she'd left off.

Mike stood on a chair, wiggling a framed landscape into place on a little hanger that had been driven into the wall. The painting showed the sweeping, chamiso-dotted hills of the local landscape with blue, jagged mountains and all the clear, hot sky in the universe above them. You had to stare at it awhile to figure out exactly what it was, but the more you looked, the more you liked. If you looked long enough you could begin to feel the heat of that unseen sun.

Roberta Vale wandered in as Mike came down from the chair and stepped back to view his handiwork.

Roberta was in a linen suit with a ruffly blouse under it—almost formal attire compared to what the rest of us wore—and in it she seemed quite cool and comfortable. She had reached an age where her beauty, without a touch of sex in it, was still beautiful; with Phyllis Upton, you were always diverting your eyes, but with Roberta you kept looking at her just to give yourself a treat.

She stepped alongside Mike and joined him in looking at the painting. "I'll be damned," she said, in that voice of hers, which I can only describe as a purring female baritone. Put Lauren Bacall's tones together with Katherine Hepburn's diction and you've got it. "That's good, Mike. *Very* good."

"It is?" asked Mike.

"You know it is," she said. "And please don't tell me you don't know anything about art but you know what you like and don't like. When somebody said that to Whistler he caustically remarked that it was a privilege shared with the lower animals. Where's the young lady who painted this?"

"Around somewhere," Mike said vaguely. "Probably haggling with the manager over the commission he's supposed to get."

"Sordid," said Roberta. "Artists should be free of that. They get the dirty end of the stick in our society."

"They do?" said Mike.

"We're too materialistic," Roberta said. "We admire only that which is designed to trick other people into giving us money. When that is the original purpose of a work of art, it is not a work of art any longer."

"Is that why there are so many starving artists?"

"No, but it's why there are so many prosperous imitation artists. Those who show us the world the way we want to see it, not the way it really is. It applies to motion pictures, which are, or should be, works of art. Truth—that's the key to it. The real truth that lies behind the apparent truth."

Mike smiled a little. His smile, in his battered face, always took on a curiously bashful, elfin quality. "Roberta, you're starting to sound like Peter Revelstoke."

"I am, aren't I?" said Roberta, laughing. "But his taste—quite correct, mind you—is an acquired thing he forces upon himself, the way Cinderella's sister tried to get into that shoe that didn't really fit. In the last analysis, Revelstoke is a purveyor of bullshit."

"Now we're beginning to agree on something," Mike said.

"Have I ever told you my index of the world?"

"Huh?" said Mike.

"The world," Roberta went on blithely, "is covered with a layer of bullshit, approximately six feet deep. Two percent of the population spends its time trying to remove it, eight percent keeps adding to it, and the other ninety percent doesn't even know this is going on."

Mike laughed heartily. "I take it back, Roberta; Revelstoke could never come up with anything like that."

"The painting," said Roberta, nodding at the wall. "I'll take it."

"Why . . . thanks, Roberta. Meredy'll be happy about that."

"She's nice," Roberta said. "You hang on to her."

"I mean to," Mike said.

The impromptu exhibit in the hotel lobby was drawing just about everyone in the company as word of it spread; it was not exactly a distraction from all the violent deaths that had been plaguing us, but it did have an analgesic effect; it seemed to suggest we couldn't surrender ourselves to horror but had to make at least a few gestures toward a normally pleasant existence. It's hard to explain how we felt—in some respects normal but in others faintly in a daze—and it was even more puzzling to endure it at the time. There was ambivalence in it. On one hand, we wanted to flee from gathering clouds before a storm struck, but on the other hand most of us wanted to finish the picture no matter what the obstacles.

Anyway, among those who came to squint at the paintings was Sam Rubicoff, the stunt coordinator, with his barrel chest and hairy arms and fierce, piratical eye. There are very few men who can wear a gold ring in the pierced lobe of one ear without making it somewhat noticeable. Sam seemed as though he'd been born with his.

He glared at one of Meredy's less realistic paintings, sighed, shook his head, and said, "George, just so nobody would think me a crude, uncultured bastard—which I probably am—I've made an honest effort to understand crap like this, but I'm damned if I do."

I shrugged. "Okay. By law you're not required to."

"That's what I always thought. But I don't want Roberta to regard me as some kind of hopeless Neanderthal."

"Roberta? What's she got to do with it?"

"Nothing, really. Just that we're damn good friends. I don't know why. She's a real lady and she's got a coupla years on me, but, hell, we just seem to get along.

Except when it comes to this kind of shit." He nodded at the painting.

"Well, I'm glad you're here," I said. "For other reasons." I looked around, wondering where Mike had disappeared to, and seeing that he was elsewhere—the bar or the men's room, for a guess—I beckoned to Sam and led him to one side. "Sam," I said, "I've been so busy I haven't had time to keep up with it—haven't even had time to ask Mike about it—so I might as well check with you."

"About what?"

"Did Mike speak to you about Joel's accident in the jeep?"

"Oh, that." He nodded. "Yeah. Mike wanted to know if anybody had been asking me how to blow up a jeep with a time delay. I told him no. Besides, I wouldn't give out information like that even if somebody did ask. These things are professional secrets."

I nodded. "Another blind alley, I guess. Mike and I had an idea Joel's accident was arranged—but I suppose we could be wrong."

Sam looked thoughtful and inhaled deeply, so that his chest expanded and took up most of the room in our immediate vicinity. "Maybe you're not so damn wrong at that," he said.

"Yeah? Why not?" In a script I hate lines that make me into a straight man, but in real life they're sometimes unavoidable.

"There's something I didn't tell Mike when he talked to me because I just didn't think of it at the time. Then, later, when I remembered, I got busy and couldn't get to him. In fact, I thought I'd mention it now if I should run into Mike."

"I'm not sure what you're talking about—but I guess that's normal, the way everything's been going lately."

"Look, George," he said, fixing his fierce eyes upon me, "maybe a week ago, or thereabouts, I went to my tin shack out on the set. You know—where I keep my explosives. The padlock was open as though somebody

125

had picked it. I thought maybe I'd carelessly left it open—and that's still possible. I checked the explosives inside and a few were missing. Special charges I use to simulate blowing things up—plenty of noise and smoke but not the force of real explosions. I've worked with enough special effects men to do all this myself when I lay out a stunt. You see, how you set 'em off in time delay is with a simple mechanism made from a relatively cheap watch—"

"Never mind the technical aspects," I said. "What counts is that somebody evidently *did* get hold of the stuff. If so, Joel may have been murdered—"

"By who? What for?" He was staring.

"I don't know. None of this makes sense. Which is why, I think, it's so damned scary. If the killer's such a complete nut he doesn't need reasons, then any one of us, at random—and for no damn reason—could be next!"

Sam shook his head and lumbered off, and a little while later Mike returned—he'd ducked into the cantina for a quick one—and I told him what I'd just learned.

Mike and I found a far corner of the lobby behind a potted cactus where there were two studded rawhide chairs. I sensed that Mike needed me for a sounding board and resigned myself to another session of playing the straight man.

"What really bothers me," said Mike, working all the lines and wrinkles in his face until they seemed to be massaging themselves, "is how we have a different M.O. with each killing. A knife...poison...a gun twice...and now a time bomb. A special effect—more a big firecracker than a bomb. It didn't kill Joel in itself, and it didn't leave any damage on the jeep that could be noticed. If we hadn't been right behind Joel nobody ever would have known there *was* an explosion. As far as I can tell, Cruz still doesn't know and believes that Joel got drunk and killed himself by crashing."

With no particular bit of dialogue in mind I merely grunted, and Mike acknowledged that with a nod and continued.

"But I'm wondering now," Mike continued, "if all these different M.O.'s don't tell us something about the murderer. You notice I'm assuming one murderer for all the victims. That's because several murderers deciding to do their stuff all at about the same time would be just too much in the way of coincidence—even harder to believe than what's already happened, and, God knows, that's hard enough to accept, as is."

"Uh huh," I said.

"So what we may have here," Mike said earnestly, "is one very clever murderer with a kind of a split personality which enables him to shift M.O.'s deliberately, probably to throw us off the track. From what, I don't know. From his real purpose, I guess, whatever that may be."

"Mike," I said, "you're getting nowhere. You know that, don't you?"

"I know it," he growled. "But it's better than not moving at all. Let me see if I can clarify this—for myself as much as for you. George, all murderers are nuts, in a way. I don't mean the insanity defense sometimes used in court, but simply that to deliberately take someone's life is, in our society, extremely abnormal behavior. Maybe all of us get the desire to do it on occasion, but very few of us act on that desire. If we do, our brain has gone wild—temporarily or as a chronic condition. Got that so far?"

"Yeah. What am I supposed to do with it?"

"Use it to realize who we're looking for. Somebody with a split personality. Split? In the case of this sonofabitch it's positively shattered."

"Okay. What's next? Give everybody a Rorschach test or something?"

"I wish to hell we could," sighed Mike. "All we can do is look for little signs. If there are any. With some types of paranoiacs—who are apt to be very intelligent, by the way—there just aren't any symptoms. Not until their fuses go off, anyway."

I frowned. "We're right back where we started."

"I wouldn't say that," Mike answered. "At least we have some facts that might show us a pattern at any time. We have even narrowed down the list of possible suspects. The passengers on the Citation executive jet, and those who took a commercial flight. Chances are, the killer was in L.A. when Spitalny was murdered."

My frown became heavier. "Mike, there may be a suspect on that list you haven't included in your thinking so far. Don't get sore now; I'm doing like cops always do and looking at *everybody* as a suspect. I'm thinking of Meredy."

"What the hell do you mean, you're thinking of Meredy?"

"I told you not to get sore. She checked with the airline for you, right? To find out who'd gone to L.A. *She* could have been on that same list—and just left herself off!"

"I'll be goddamned," said Mike, glowering at me. "They do well casting you as a cop sometimes. You're mean enough to be one."

Sunday morning.

Except in very rare cases, the makers of motion pictures do not work on Sundays. Neither God nor the union likes it. Phyllis had considered asking for Sunday work just to gain some time but had finally decided the custom was too sacred to violate even in the desperate situation, time-wise and budget-wise, in which we found ourselves.

So here it was Sunday, and here I was, at the airport, going over my Cessna 182, and trying to figure out which of its instruments I could remove in order to put in a Loran C navigator. I've already got enough instrumentation to take a Boeing 747 from here to West Hell and back, but that's part of the pleasure of owning an airplane. The electronics guy at Van Nuys airport, where I keep it, had this Loran that was a good buy and I wanted it. Needed it. Wanted it. I don't know, maybe they were the same thing—in my mind, anyway.

As I sat there in the Cessna, in front of the hangar,

taking measurements on the instrument panel with an ordinary ruler, I saw the Citation jet trundle out to the end of the runway. I switched on my radio and heard Ferdinand Holtz getting his clearance from the tower.

Some of you may be old enough to remember a radio comedian named Jack Pearl who called himself Baron Munchausen. He would tell these tall tales and when his stooge expressed disbelief he would always say, "Vass you dere, Sharley?" What made it funny was the accent. Well, Ferdy Holtz sounded just like that old comedian. There were times when you thought he had to be putting it on, just for comic relief.

Ferdy was flying this Sunday morning because we'd worked late the day before and he was taking the dailies back. The lab in L.A. had agreed to process them during weekend hours for an overtime fee that probably gave Phyllis another sleepless night.

I knew that Roberta Vale was Ferdy's only passenger this trip, and, being Roberta, she was probably in the cockpit with him, learning how the damned thing worked. Since she wouldn't be on call for a couple of days, Roberta was returning to L.A. to catch up on some personal business, part of which was to get some opinions from fellow art lovers on the painting she had just bought from Meredy.

Meredy had sold four of her paintings at the exhibition in the hotel lobby, among them a bullfight scene Glenn Ford had taken a fancy to. It was another of her semi-abstractions; you couldn't exactly see either the bull or the matador, but somehow you could smell the blood.

"You are cleared for immediate takeoff," the tower said to Ferdy in a Spanish accent almost as thick as Ferdy's German accent. I don't know how they understood each other.

The Citation rolled. I watched it because it was beautiful. That's my idea of art: an airplane taking off or landing. Maybe, I thought, Meredy Ames might be able to capture the real feeling of an aircraft reaching for the sky in paint and canvas. If she could, I'd buy it.

Halfway down the runway, the small jet wobbled, and although I sensed that something was wrong I didn't want to believe it—not in that first instant, anyway, because it is so seldom that, with such a fine airplane and such an experienced pilot, anything goes wrong.

Instead of waiting until he was completely airborne, Ferdy practically pulled his landing gear up from the runway itself. The airplane gained a few feet of altitude, not so much from the manipulation of its control surfaces as from its forward speed, which had the effect of making it want to fly. I couldn't imagine why, at this point, Ferdy didn't pull the nose up and let her reach for the sky.

And then—in the next microsecond—I had a flash memory of Ferdy, the last time I'd flown with him, having a chest pain that could have come from an over-spiced enchilada or could have been a cardiac glitch with a long Latin name. I didn't exactly have time to think about this, but the airplane I was watching was acting as though its pilot was having a heart attack.

I stared.

The airplane was almost at the end of the runway now. Its nose dropped. My heart dropped with it. My eyes widened with disbelief. Instead of climbing, the Citation slammed itself downward at a shallow angle. It struck the rough desert ground just beyond the runway. I saw a ball of flame—like a bright orange with its charred skin peeling away—and the glob of black smoke that formed over it and rolled up into the air. I heard the sound of the explosion and seemed to feel its concussion even at this distance.

I piled out of my own parked airplane and started running toward the wreck.

A crash truck was already heading for it, red lights flashing.

CHAPTER ELEVEN

In a motion picture you can indicate the passage of painful
and bewildering hours by jumping from one scene to the
next, but in real life you've got to put up with that in-
tervening time no matter how unpleasant it might be.
Two hours after the crash I was still at the airport. In the
hot sunlight, at the end of the runway, the scattered pieces
of the wreck were still smoking. A guard of khaki-clad
policemen surrounded the area. An ambulance was out
there and orderlies from it were poking around, looking
for bodies, but not finding any—only small pieces. I had
been on the phone, meanwhile, and I knew that back at
the hotel, Phyllis, as shocked by the news as everyone
else, was frantically busy sending out notifications and
relaying word of this latest disaster to all parties concerned.

I was partly stunned; I think everybody in the company must have been upon receiving word of the crash.
Mike Corby suddenly appeared beside me without a noticeable approach; the way characters suddenly pop up
in dreams. Each of us must have muttered some kind of
greeting, but, for the life of me, I have no memory of
it.

"George, I need your help." I remember Mike saying
that much. He followed it with a long explanation, which
I vaguely absorbed. The explanation involved Meredy—
and I suddenly realized that she, too, was on hand, and
had evidently accompanied Mike here. "She has some
leverage with Cruz," Mike said; "she can make the request in fluent Spanish, which ought to cut more ice with
him."

My thoughts were like complete litter on top of a desk; I was still trying to sort everything out when, shortly afterward, Mike and I walked out toward the smoking remains of the airplane with Captain of Detectives Alfonso Cruz, Mike with his usual rolling, bantam-rooster stride, Cruz with his curious fat man's grace, and I in my ursine shamble.

It was only then that it became absolutely clear to me that I was supposed to assist in what amounted to an investigation. Cruz, under Meredy's blandishments, had reluctantly agreed to take us both out to the wreck, but, as we approached it, he was still grumbling.

"Senor Corby," he said to Mike, through a suspicious scowl, "you promised you would stop interfering—no?"

"And I'm not," said Mike. "I'm bringing my suspicions directly to you this time. Cards on the table."

"Why now, so suddenly?"

"Because it's the only way I can get a look at the plane."

"Perhaps. But you are not to touch anything. The aviation officials are the only persons authorized to do that when they get here from Mexico City."

"I know," said Mike. "But if they're not looking for something in particular, they may not find it. And if we *do* find anything, it's all yours. As the officer in charge of the investigation, you get all the credit."

Cruz was thoughtful for a moment as we continued walking. "Senor Corby, you say it is possible someone tampered with the airplane, causing it to crash. You wish Senor Kennedy, who is an expert on airplanes, to take a look."

"That's right. If only to eliminate the possibility. Actually, George here thinks it's more likely the pilot had something like a heart attack during takeoff. Apparently he had some physical trouble along those lines and was hiding it. If so, this terrible accident came at an unfortunate time—following a series of apparent homicides. But it's those homicides that make it necessary for us to be very sure that this airplane crash isn't one of them—do you see what I mean?"

"With some difficulty," said Cruz dryly, his ripe-olive eyes hiding whatever black amusement he was feeling. "It seems to me that this suspicion of yours comes out of the air. You must have more reason for it than—what is the word?—than a hunch, no?"

Mike drew a deep breath and let it out again. "Captain," he said, "I might as well level with you. All the way. This airplane crash might not be an accident for the same reason that Joel Totterelli's jeep overturning was probably not an accident."

Cruz halted and stared at Mike. "What? What is this you are saying now?"

Mike quickly explained the explosion we'd seen before the jeep went off the road, and our subsequent talks with Sam Rubicoff, the stunt coordinator, who believed some of his explosives had been stolen. "I didn't report this to you before," said Mike, "because you weren't in a mood to be talked to, and I didn't want it to get out before we finished our location shooting. Now I have to take a chance. All I can do is hope you won't spread it around. Not until we're all packed up and out of here for good."

"That," said Cruz, "is a day I am looking forward to."

With the wreckage of the Citation scattered over such a wide area, I did not think I would find anything significant, and, as it turned out, I did not. Cruz hovered over me during the inspection to be sure I did no more than look, and refrained from touching anything. Afterward, the three of us returned to the small lunch counter in the airport passenger building and had coffee, while Cruz surrounded us with clouds of smoke from one of his foul cigarettes.

"Okay," I said, summing it up. "You have to realize I'm not an expert on crash investigation, and I'm not checked out in the Citation. So I could be wrong. But based on a general knowledge of airplanes, and on what little I could see of the wreckage, I can report that I didn't find anything that struck me as out of place. I don't think the airplane was tampered with. I think something happened to the pilot. A sudden heart attack—something along those lines."

Mike nodded. "That still leaves a nasty possibility. What if Ferdy had been poisoned? A slow-acting poison of some kind, dropped into his coffee—" he shook his head abruptly. "Too far out," he said. "Listen to me— getting weird ideas. I ought to know better. It's just that this whole thing's been so damned weird and far out right from the beginning—"

"On that much we agree, Senor," said Cruz. "Is it one killer, from the beginning? If so, what is the motive? We could perhaps find separate motives for each of the murders, but what motive fits them all?"

"Could be just to hurt the picture," I said. "To keep it from ever getting finished."

"And who might wish to do that?" There was almost a touch of sarcasm in Cruz's voice.

"I don't know." I shrugged. "J. Sutton Fargo, for twisted moralistic reasons, even if he is an investor? Peter Revelstoke as the ultimate snob, off his rocker and ready to kill for it? Somebody who hates one of us enough to ruin the whole picture, just so we can't succeed if it gets finished. How the hell do I know?"

"En punto," said Cruz smugly. "You do not know, and I do not know either."

"Which puts us right back at square one," said Mike. He sipped coffee.

Cruz lit another cigarette and made even thicker clouds of smoke.

I was convinced that the crash of the Citation, in which both Ferdy Holtz and Roberta Vale had died, was an accident—one that might have happened even if there hadn't been a series of apparent murders preceding it. But the effect it had on everyone was just the same as the reactions another murder might have produced. Although Phyllis somehow talked everyone into continuing with the shooting, I could see that no one liked it, and that very few members of either the cast or the crew could really concentrate on their jobs.

Because I was directing now, and in various ways concerned with most of the members of the company, many of them were expressing their discontent to me. A number of the actors and actresses had finished their work and left, but the few who remained were still immensely important to the picture. We couldn't afford to lose one of them in a walkout that might even be justified. Some came close to walking out.

"I'm not superstitious," said Mariette Hartley, frowning, "but with everybody dying this way, what can we think?"

"I don't want to ruin the picture," said Glenn Ford, "but if one more person gets knocked off—well, what else can I say?"

"It's a good thing I only have one more scene," said Dean Martin, "or I'd leave right now."

Jennifer Schwartz, her clipboard tight to her breast and her eyes open wide, said, "George, I'm scared!"

"Know something?" I answered. "So am I."

The next delay in the shooting was one already anticipated and budgeted for. There was a sequence earlier in the story where the young cowhand, played by rock star Alex Keglmeyer, rode a wild steer down the main street of the town in order to call attention to himself. His ride made him smash everything in sight, knocking down posts that supported overhead canopies, demolishing store-front windows and porches, and even toppling the water tower that supplied the locomotive at the station. If this episode had been shot chronologically, the whole set would have had to have been rebuilt, as, presumably, the town was in the story. So it had to be done, instead, when we were finished with those parts of the set that would be destroyed. And each shot in the sequence had to be done right the first time. Retakes would mean reconstruction, which was out of the question. But a certain amount of remodeling—if it may be called that—had to be accomplished before any of the takes could be filmed. Whatever was supposed to break when the rider of the wild steer (who would be a stunt man) crashed into it had to be made of breakaway material, such as balsa. The windows that were to be shattered would also be of a special glass that wouldn't break into sharp pieces or injure the stunt man severely. To insert all the breakaway parts would take two days, and they were scheduled adjacent to the weekend so that we'd all have a breather.

I thought, upon returning to L.A., that I'd have a good, long stretch at home all to myself, where, as paterfamilias, I could solve all the domestic problems a house full of young persons seems to generate, and even find a little time to plan the installation of some new and expensive instrumentation in my airplane. About those problems. They're not really problems, and I don't really solve them. They have to do with everything from record collections of that god-awful music to what clothes to wear at graduation parties. The kids don't feel right about them until they lay them on my lap, and then I say something—anything, really—and they go away satisfied, at least until the next problem.

I was all set for such a turbulent rest when J. Sutton Fargo phoned and insisted that I have lunch with him and Marilou at Ma Maison.

We got a wall table not too near the center of things, but from which Marilou Fargo could have a good view of all the movie people who might drop in. She was dressed as though for an event, though quietly enough and in good taste. Her darkish suit slimmed down her pigeon-plump figure somewhat. The diamond on her engagement ring must have made it a little more difficult for her to lift her left hand. From the way her hair was absolutely in place, I imagined she must have spent all morning at the beauty shop.

"Jo-werdge," she said, her eyes roving in excitement, "isn't that Robert Redford over there?"

"Sure is," I said.

"Maybe he'd like to come over here and have a drink with us."

"He's probably got a business discussion, same as we have," I said as diplomatically as I could. I looked at Fargo. "Uh—this is business, I take it?"

Fargo showed the amiable smile that didn't match the wariness of his eyes. He'd acquired it, I thought, along with his Brooks Brothers suit and all those oil wells. "Business and pleasure," he said. "'Bout half and half. Some folks say you shouldn't mix the two, but I don't go 'long with that."

"And Meryl Streep!" said Marilou, blinking toward the entrance, where the maître d' was escorting a party to a table.

"That's not Meryl," I said, glancing. "It's somebody who looks like her. I don't know who it is."

"Oh," said Marilou, disappointed.

"Marilou," said Fargo, "I don't know why you get yourself so stirred up over these movie stars. They're just people. They put their pants on the same as anybody else does."

"They're not like other people, Sut," she said. "They wouldn't be movie stars if they were."

He frowned a little. "Maybe, they're different, at that."

"In some ways," I said, shrugging. "This being recognized wherever you go gets to you after a while. You start sitting in restaurants with your back to the room, so you won't be bothered. Not that it's that much bother, though. The fans are important. They're who keep you up there."

"I was thinking of what it leads to," said Fargo, "getting rich and famous real quick, the way movie stars do. Now, you take my case. I'm not famous—except maybe in a limited way in financial circles—but I am, as you know, pretty well-off. I didn't get that way all at once. I had a chance to get used to it as it came along."

"You must be driving at something," I said, "but I'm damned if I know what it is."

"Let me start at the beginning here," he said, "just so you know exactly what's on my mind. I figured you were the one to discuss it with, because you appear to have your head screwed on right. We're all of us born with Satan in our hearts, you know, and he's right there, with all of his temptations, as long as we live. Has to be fought all the time. Can't let down your guard even a minute."

"I guess that's one way to put it," I said, noncommittally. Once, when I was doing a Navy picture, I was a dinner guest in the ward room of an aircraft carrier. On the menu it said, "Gentlemen will refrain from discussing politics, ladies, or religion." I've always thought it was good advice.

"Now, when these movie people get rich quick, the way they do," continued Fargo, "they find they can suddenly afford all the temptations they've always really wanted, and it's just too much for 'em. They lose control. Start to cheat on their husbands and wives. Get divorces. Drink too much. Smoke marihuana and go on to harder drugs. It's only a little step from that to serious crime. And right on up the ladder to the ultimate crime—murder."

"Sut," I said, trying to be serious and sensible, "you just can't lay this kind of thing on movie people in particular."

"All you have to do is read the news," he said. "Nice gal like Natalie Wood fallin' off the boat to drown while everybody else was havin' a drinkin' party on that there boat. And John Belushi dyin' of an overdose, if that's what really happened. Marilyn Monroe—they still say there's a mystery about how she died. All these big stars up on narcotics charges—a new one every week, I swear. If they hadn't been in the movie business, with sin all around 'em, like weeds in a cabbage patch, none o' this ever would have happened to 'em."

"We can't be sure of that. Hundreds of ordinary people are having this kind of trouble every day—we just don't hear about it."

"Exactly," said Fargo.

"Exactly what?" I asked.

"Exactly the way the Communists planned it."

"The Communists?" I looked puzzled. "How did they get into this?"

"They have been deliberately eating away at our moral fiber for damn near half a century. Pushing their godless doctrines on our young people. Channeling secret funds to protestors and demonstrators. Supplyin' heroin to our GI's in Vietnam, so they'd get hooked and bring it home with them."

"Sut," I said with a deep sigh, "you can't blame just *everything* on them."

"And that's what they depend on. It's so overwhelmingly atrocious no one will believe it. But back to this movie we got on our hands. You know why I invested in it in the first place. Figured it might be a force for decency, for promotin' the old-fashioned principles that made us a great nation. The way John Wayne's movies used to. All that seems to have backfired now."

"Backfired? It's still the same movie. We just have to finish it, that's all. Another week or two of shooting, then post-production. We're in the home stretch."

He nodded. "That's what's made me hesitate to withdraw my support. Seemed a shame to do it so near the end. But I'm a businessman, George, and I've been in this kind of situation before. Somethin' gets almost finished before you finally realize you've made a bad investment. Thing to do, then, is get out fast. Take your loss, and don't add any more to it."

"*The Godless* is not a bad investment," I said, tapping the table with my forefinger. "It'll gross beautifully. Maybe even break box-office records. I've been with it from the start, and I've seen almost all the dailies. Just

take my word for it, it's great. Maybe the greatest western ever made."

"Possibly. From an artistic standpoint. But I've
learned a lot since I jumped into this, perhaps too im-
pulsively, or perhaps—" (he showed a dry smile) "because Marilou, here, was buggin' me to do it. One of
the things I learned was that a motion picture can very
well be an artistic triumph and a box-office disaster.
That's the business aspect. The other aspect—the moral
aspect, which I feel very deeply—is also backfiring.
These murders have begun to symbolize all the depravity
of the Hollywood scene, which the public, who worships
motion-picture people like the golden calves they are,
will be inclined to emulate. If those folks in Hollywood
can get away with it, they'll say, so can we."

I frowned. "But, all these conclusions of yours are
pretty iffy. You've got to admit that."

"I'm aware of it. Any investment has an element of
risk, and is, as you say, iffy. You make decisions on the
basis of whatever data you can gather. Usually it's hard
data—the result of analysis or marketing information—
that sort of thing. But I have a strong religious conviction,
George, and I also rely on signs. I don't know how it
works, but God himself very often gives me signs about
whether or not to do something. It's a question of learning
to read them."

"You've had some kind of sign on this?"

"The murders are a sign," he said firmly. "They're
a warning. God is tellin' me to back off."

"What if it's not that? What if it turns out that the
murders have a perfectly rational explanation? Mike Corby's working on them, you know, and he just might get
to the bottom of it before we're through."

Fargo shrugged. "That's possible. Anything is possible. I'm not sayin' I'm a hundred percent right. But
I'm surer'n hell somewhere up in the high-nineties. Anyway, I've just about made my decision."

"Which is?"

Marilou Fargo, who had been sipping some kind of

fruity cocktail through a straw and munching on some kind of triple-decker sandwich, interrupted us. "Look!" she said. "It's Clint Eastwood! He's comin' over here, I think!"

I looked up. It was Clint, all right, smiling at me as he approached. His well-tailored business suit was almost a disguise. He arrived at the table and said, "Hi, George. How ya doin'?"

"Fine. How's yourself? Sit down."

"I'll only be a minute." He laughed a little. "I don't usually table-hop, but this was a good chance to catch you."

"I'd like you to meet Sut Fargo, here, and Marilou Fargo."

"Well, how do you do," said Marilou, offering her hand. "I've always wanted to meet you. You don't look at all like you do on the screen. I mean, the way you're dressed up. May I call you Clint?"

"Of course." He looked at Fargo. "You must be the gentleman who's helping to back *The Godless*. We need more like you."

"Well, I understand money's hard to raise these days. I'm still not sure I did the right thing. George and I have just been discussin' it."

"I know what it's like," said Clint, with a grin. "Especially since I've been producing my own pictures." He turned his attention to me. "That's what I wanted to drop in your ear, George. I've got a project on the fire. The property's an earlier novel by the same guy who wrote *The Godless*. Science-fiction yarn called, *I, the Unspeakable*."

"Yeah," I said. "I read it. Pretty good."

"Remember the big politician who was in charge of everything in the future world, where everybody had numbers instead of names? Hell of a part for you. I kept seeing you in it when I read it."

"A bad guy again, huh?" I was grinning too. "Like in *Thunderbolt and Lightfoot*."

"You're the best bad guy I know," he said. "Anyway,

I thought I'd check to see if you were interested. If you are, I'll have my agent get in touch with yours."

"Fine. Sure you won't have a drink?"

"Busy, busy, busy," he said. "See you later, George. Nice meeting you, Marilou and Sut."

When he had spun away, Marilou said, "Why, he's absolutely charming!"

"They all are," said Fargo, a shade sourly. He turned to me again. "We were talkin' about money for *The Godless*."

"I know we were. Your decision."

"Phyllis Upton's gonna ask me for another two million. I know that through the grapevine. She can't get it from the banks—they're not gonna throw good money after bad. Well, neither am I. You can tell her that if you will, George. Not another nickel."

I noticed that as Fargo said this his eyes seemed to flare and his lips seemed to tremble. It was an extremely subtle facial expression which maybe only an actor, who is always observing facial expressions, might have noticed. I had a wild thought—and knew it was wild even as it came to me. Mike and I, discussing the murders, had already speculated that maybe we were looking for a nut, which would explain the apparent lack of rational motivation. In this moment, J. Sutton Fargo seemed to me a species of nut. There was nothing else to connect him with the murders—I had no idea how he would check out time-and-place-wise—but as a very rich man he could probably arrange to be anywhere, anytime, largely unobserved, or even hire a person, or persons, unknown to do his dirty work for him.

None of this added up, in my mind, to a full accusation, or even a strong suspicion. But it was there, as another possibility. And I was a little ashamed of it until I realized I'd probably be ashamed of suspecting anybody, even the real murderer, at this stage of the game.

"Sut," I said, frowning, "you can't just let the whole thing die for what is a relatively small amount—and forgive me for calling it that. Two million makes my head swim, but it's still only around five percent of the total. That's not an excessive cost overrun."

"My mind's made up," he said.

"If Mike could solve these murders," I persisted, "if all this publicity about them would die out—couldn't you maybe change your mind?"

"I don't know," said Fargo. Little dots of sweat appeared just over his eyebrows as he worked them in a kind of kneading motion, obviously in great discomfort and maybe even in some kind of mental pain. "I just don't know about that. . . ."

The food is great at Ma Maison, but I still didn't enjoy the rest of my lunch that day.

The bedside phone rang just when I thought I was getting to sleep. Joan answered and, with a patient expression, she said, "It's for you," and handed me the phone.

It was no hour for a cheerful hello, so I growled, "Yeah?"

"It's Mike," said Mike's voice, coming through a barrier of static. "I had a hell of a time making the connection from here."

"Then you must be in Chirapulco. Though it sounds to me like you're in Tibet or someplace."

"I might as well be, for all I've got to work with here. Look, George, I've started a file. On the murders, I mean. Like I would have had when I was a cop—only not as elaborate. Every suspect gets a jacket, and all the dope I get on said suspect goes into it. Got the idea?"

Joan, who is almost as tall as I am, stretched out languidly to return to the sleep she was enjoying and muttered, "Wake me if you need me."

"Yeah, I know. It's how murders are really solved. You've told me a million times. Did you ring me up in the middle of the night to make it a million and one?"

Joan smiled and murmured, "You're teed off, George. Your voice gets very sweet when you're teed off."

I shushed her with a gesture.

"I need stuff that I can't get here for the file," Mike continued. "One thing is police records. Yellow sheets, like we used to say at NYPD. On every possible suspect. George, what I want you to do is see Ollie Kingsley at LAPD. He already knows you, so he'll cooperate. At least I think he will, unless he's still sore about what we did when we found Spitalny's body. I'm going to give you a list of names, and I want you to ask Ollie to run 'em through R and I. That's Records and Identification—"

"I know. I've played enough cops to know that much."

"Well, don't try to play cop or anything on this one. Just get what you can, and bring it back for me, okay?"

"Okay, okay." I shuffled straight in bed. "Joan, you're the crossword puzzle fan around here; got a pencil?"

She waved sleepily at the bedside table and I saw one there atop the newspaper puzzle she'd been doing. I hoped I'd remember to put it back so there wouldn't be a crisis in the morning.

When I hit his office early the next morning, pipe-smoking Captain Oliver Kingsley wasn't quite as cordial as he'd been last time. He was polite, to be sure—offered me coffee and all that—but his smile seemed a little forced and he kept looking at me sideways.

He studied the list of names I gave him. "Lotta people here. Looks like your whole cast and crew down there."

"Not quite that," I said. "I think it's basically everybody who could have been on hand when the murders were committed."

"I'll assume Mike knows what he's doing. But I must say I have some sympathy for this guy, Cruz, down in Chirapulco. I know what it's like when outsiders start messing in an investigation."

"Oh, you know about Cruz?"

"Of course. The murders—Cruz—how you all got jailed—what Mike's been up to—everything. Who doesn't know? Every news medium from the big networks to neighborhood weeklies has picked up the story. To say nothing of scuttlebutt when cops throughout the country gather at their coffee machines. Looks like Mike

144

bit off more than he can chew this time. If he solves the murders, fine—he's a hero. But do you know what the chances against that are? You'd have to be an astronomer to grasp the numbers."

"I think Mike realizes that. Just the same he's gotta do it. Climbing Everest because it's there, and all that."

"Has he thought what'll happen if he doesn't get anywhere? To his own career, I mean."

"We've both thought about it. If it turns out he took on the investigation and then blew it, his reputation as a sharp cop is gone. Never mind all the good work he once did—in this town they just want to know what you've done *lately*. And, let's face it, Mike's not a superb actor, he's an interesting character, which gives him a little box-office pull, and that's why they cast him. If the fans start to think he's a phony, he won't get any more work. And, between you and me, captain, I think he needs it."

Kingsley nodded. "He may find it hard to get police work, too. Well, I'll run these names through R and I if that'll help. Doubt it will, though. I suppose you need 'em right away."

"Yesterday would be nice."

"You'll have to settle for tomorrow. Even those computers at the FBI in Washington, which are supposed to contain records of all arrests nationwide, get overloaded. They also goof once in a while. Furthermore, I'm going to have to sneak this one in. It's hardly our jurisdiction."

"Ollie," I said, "I realize it's an imposition. But I know Mike will appreciate it. He owes you a case of scotch or something."

"Tell him I drink bourbon," said Kingsley, putting another kitchen match to his pipe, which had gone out. That's the thing about pipes; they're always going out.

CHAPTER TWELVE

Mike fidgeted as he sat in the big room that served as Meredy Ames's living quarters and studio. She was at her easel, painting. Near the window, where the light streamed inside, stood Luis Mondragon, whose professional bullfighting name was *El Alacrán*, the Scorpion. Dressed in his suit of lights, and with his cape thrown over one shoulder, Luis was striking an arrogant pose.

Mike looked at his watch. "Come on, Meredy. The afternoon's disappearing. It'll never come again."

"Just a few more touches," said Meredy. "I can't stop now."

Mike sighed deeply.

Again, I am reporting upon a brief episode I didn't witness personally. But, again, since both Mike and Meredy told me about it later, I think I've got it right. Right enough to report on, anyway.

Mike, in a sedan he'd commandeered, had driven out to Meredy's *jacal* to pick her up and bring her back to his hotel room. Not for hanky-panky. They could have had all the hanky-panky they wanted at her place, or his place, or any of a number of places. What they planned this time was much more serious, or, at any rate, more business than pleasure. Meredy had volunteered to help Mike put his files together—type his scribbled notes and arrange everything neatly. A woman of many parts—bartender and painter, to begin—she had secretarial experience from the time she'd run the office as a front for her ex-husband's bunco games.

But right now she was all artist, as she squinted at the posing bullfighter and daubed away vigorously at the canvas. She wore patched and faded blue denim overalls. They'd have looked baggy on anyone else, but Meredy gave them a certain flair. At least, to Mike's eye, she did.

"Luis," she said, "could you raise your hand on your hip a little more, the way it was? That's it. Thank you."

"Maybe I better go on back to the hotel," said Mike.

"No, no—stay right where you are. Another minute or two."

"You've been saying that for the last fifteen minutes."

"Be patient, Mike. Aren't cops supposed to be patient?"

"Not this patient," said Mike, scowling.

He was trying to understand Meredy's side of it, and succeeding only partly at this. Luis, he understood, had commissioned her to do the portrait, and this was probably her first actual commission. He ought not to blame her for seeing the portrait as the most important business at hand, no matter what else needed to be done.

And he had to admit that Luis, in his pose, seemed a good subject for a painting. Mike hadn't any idea how good he was as a bullfighter—probably far from the top, since he was still in the bush league out here in Chirapulco—but he certainly looked the part. The spangles and embroidery on his costume glittered, and Mike supposed that was why it was called a suit of lights. He was a slim, well-favored youth and his eyes were large, dark and soulful; there was a look of suffering in them as though he'd just been carried out of the ring, wounded.

"Take a break, Luis," said Meredy, stepping back to look at her work.

The young matador smiled, came out of his pose, and stretched himself. "It is worse than the *recibiendo*," he said.

Meredy laughed. "I can see where it is."

"What's the *recibiendo?*" asked Mike.

"One of two ways to kill the bull," explained Meredy. "You either come forward or you stand perfectly still and receive him. Receiving—the *recibiendo*—is much more difficult. It requires the greatest of courage."

"Someday I will do it," Luis said, smiling shyly. "Someday, when I have the right bull for it."

"Yes," said Meredy. "You'll be great, Luis. I have a feeling you will."

"There is much luck in it." Luis shrugged slightly. "You must be good, of course, but then you need some luck on top of that. I said this many times to my good friend, Wally, before he died. He wanted so much to be an actor, you know."

"So I understood," said Meredy.

Luis turned his soulful eyes on Mike. "Is it true what I have heard, Senor Corby? Was Wally really murdered?"

"I can't say for sure, Luis," said Mike. "Just that there's some indication of that. You—uh—wouldn't know anything about it, would you?"

"What would I know? I saw him the night before he died. We sat for a while in *El Pichon Azul*, and we talked quietly. As we did many times. He left early, saying he needed his sleep for his jump in the morning. That is all I know."

"Just thought I'd ask," said Mike. "It's part of trying to put it all together."

Luis nodded. "Senorita Ames has told me of your efforts. I wish I could help. If Wally was killed—and by the same person who killed the others—I would want this person brought to justice."

"If you think of anything, let me know." Mike turned to Meredy. "Ready to go now?"

She glanced at the painting, then at Mike again. "I *was* hoping for a few minutes more, but I guess the light has changed. All right, Mike; I'll knock off for now."

Mike rose from the chair and exercised his legs by wandering around the room and looking at some of Meredy's other paintings as both she and the matador changed their clothes. As a pause-filler, he said to Luis, "You speak pretty good English. Hell of a lot better than my Spanish. How did you learn?"

"I was raised in El Paso, senor," said Luis, unwinding his sash. "I suppose I would be there today had I not chosen the *corrida*. Who knows how these things happen? One day, at a corner, you turn right instead of left, and that is it. You find a new dream, and you follow it. Wally wished for me to return to the States with him. He thought perhaps I could be a stunt man, too. But I cannot leave the bullring. It is what I was meant for. With luck, I will appear in *El Capital* one of these days— perhaps even travel to Spain." He laughed slightly. "Everyone here in Chirapulco wishes to leave. It is a place of sadness, you know. There is nothing but death here for anyone who stays...."

Minutes later, both Luis and Meredy had changed their clothes and were outside, ready to depart. Meredy stepped into the sedan Mike had borrowed, and Luis started toward his TR-7 sports car, which, from the way it shone, was obviously his pride and joy. Halfway to it, he turned and came back to the sedan, leaning at the window to talk to Mike in the driver's seat.

"It may be nothing," he said. "But Senorita Ames tells me you are looking for any kind of information, even if it does not seem important, no?"

"That's right. What have you got?"

"It is not about myself and Wally. It is about the young woman who was killed just before Wally died. What was her name?"

"Trish Wainwright?"

"Yes. That is the one. She was always in *El Pichon Azul,* where she would meet Senor Mendoza y Villasenor. We saw her many times. I saw her that night. Before she was found in the arroyo."

"Well, we already know she was in the Blue Pigeon that night. It doesn't seem to mean very much."

Luis shrugged. "Perhaps not. I was thinking of the person she met outside."

"What's this, now? Who did she meet outside?"

"Let me explain. Wally and I left the cantina just a moment after Senorita Wainwright did. My car was parked outside and we were going to it. There was another car parked nearby—much like the one you are driving now; it may have been the same. Senorita Wainwright got into *this* car."

"Okay," said Mike, frowning to unravel it in his mind. "Go on."

"There was someone else in this car—the driver. It was too dark and I did not see the driver clearly. But Wally, who was with me, thought he recognized the driver. And then the car drove away."

A moment passed, and Mike said, "Yeah? What next?"

"That is all," said Luis.

"That's all? What's the point of the story?"

"I do not know. You said you were looking for any kind of information, even if it seemed to have no meaning. I thought this might have *some* meaning. Suppose the one in the car was the one who took Senorita Wainwright to the arroyo and killed her?"

"Kind of a long shot," said Mike. "But you're right; we don't want to overlook anything. Okay. You say Wally recognized the driver. Who was it?"

Luis's frown added to his look of being in pain. "I do not remember. Wally spoke some name, but I do not remember it. Nothing seemed to be wrong; there was no reason to remember it. We both forgot seeing Senorita Wainwright and went to my car and drove off."

"Then it couldn't have been a name you already know. Was it someone with the movie company?"

"I supposed it was, because of the company automobile. But I didn't ask. All of this, you might say, went into one of my ears and out the other. Perhaps I have wasted your time even to mention it—"

"No, no, that's okay," Mike said quickly. "Any information's better than no information at all. Anyway, thanks, Luis. I appreciate your interest."

"*Por nada,* senor," said the bullfighter. He swiveled off gracefully, as though twirling a cape, and stalked to his own car.

Although I had had a full day directing the scene where the town got demolished, and was looking forward to an early bedtime and to reading myself to sleep by studying the scenes to be shot in the morning, I couldn't resist wandering down the balcony to Mike's room to find out if he'd made any progress in his investigation. I'd showered and had some food sent up, so I figured I'd last another thirty minutes or so before my head went entirely numb and my thoughts, instead of staying in one place, began to come and go.

I'd already supplied Mike with the police records I'd pried from Captain Kingsley, and I knew of his plan to set up all the data he'd accumulated so far into a cross-reference system that would at least vaguely resemble the files he was used to. I didn't know whether this was something that would actually work for him, or whether it was merely one of his notions. That hardly mattered. Just having him do something—anything—about the murders somehow made me feel a little more at ease, and I was sure it did the same for him.

He opened the door when I knocked, and I saw that the room was strewn with manila file-folders into which had been inserted sheaves of paper. Meredy, looking slim, boyish, and even a little stylish in peon's trousers and an embroidered Mexican shirt that was tied like a bandana at her bare midriff, was at the hotel-room desk banging away at a portable typewriter.

"Come in, George," Mike said. "Drink?"

"No, thanks. But I'll take a coupla toothpicks to keep my eyes open."

Meredy looked up and smiled. "Rough day at the office?"

"It wasn't easy. We used multiple cameras because we couldn't shoot again for close-ups. Phyllis brought two more camera crews in just for today. There goes the budget again. I spoke to the location accountant. He says we're still in the black, but if we buy a bottle of ink to enter it we'll be in the red again A comedian. Everybody wants to be a comedian."

"Sit down," said Mike. "Relax. Let's all relax." He looked at his watch. "We can afford about ten seconds of it, at least."

I sat, enjoyed the soft cushions for a moment, then said, "Well? How's it going? Any leads yet?"

Mike picked up a long, yellow legal pad on which he'd evidently written some notes, and frowned at it. "I don't know if I'm getting closer or more confused than ever. Anyway, I now know more about our suspects than they know about themselves. Suspects? I shouldn't call 'em that yet. I just don't know what else to call 'em."

It's probable that motion-picture people run afoul of the law no more—or no less—than people anywhere else. But I had the impression that a high percentage of those whose backgrounds Mike had looked into had police records of one kind or another. I hadn't seen the police records Captain Kingsley had given me, incidentally; they had come, like a packet of porn, in a plain brown envelope which I hadn't opened on the way to Chirapulco, though I'd been tempted to.

"The first thing I've done is boil the list down," said Mike, "to those who could have been on hand, according to time and place, when all the murders were committed. This rests on two premises that could be wrong—in which case everything I've got is wrong—but you have to start somewhere, and starting with these two premises is better than starting with nothing at all. The first premise is that one person did all the killing. It's also the shakiest premise, but we'll go along with it for the time being. The second premise is that the same killer knocked off Nick Spitalny, and we don't know this for sure, either; just that Spitalny's death was coincidental as hell, coming, as it did, when we were about to pump him for information. What the Spitalny murder does is place the killer in Los Angeles at the time. What that does, in turn, is narrow the list down to those who were, or could have been, there. If we don't use this as a working hypothesis,

152

we've got practically the whole company to consider—close to two hundred people."

"Very fine lecture," I said, yawning. "I was gonna read myself to sleep, but I guess I'll sit here and listen to you instead."

"Just putting it in perspective," said Mike. "Let's take a look at a few of these upright citizens. Let's start with Ira Yoder." He glanced at his list. "Burglary, second degree. Suspicion of. They caught him in a warehouse six years ago—it was full of TV sets. He copped a plea and pleaded guilty to trespassing. Fine and suspended sentence."

"Ira? I wouldn't have pegged him as a burglar."

"Maybe he wasn't. All these yellow sheets show is the bare facts. Much too bare. Maybe he just wandered into the joint to get out of the rain and *had* to cop his plea to stay out of jail. Anyway, it was before he was established as a P.R. man, and presumably in a period of financial difficulty."

"It hardly says he's a murderer."

"Right. But it still adds a tiny piece to the jigsaw puzzle. Let's move on. Cora Foster."

"She's got a record?"

"Yeah. And it doesn't surprise me. She got herself indicted some years ago for a spiritualist scam. Evidently one of these store-front places where they summon up the ghost of your Uncle Charley and take you for all you've got. Hard to convict, and she got off, too. Blossom was a little kid then and probably didn't know much about it. So this probably doesn't mean anything when it comes to murder, either."

I frowned uncomfortably. "I'm not so sure I want to know all this. Don't ever let Jennifer Schwartz see that list."

"Funny you should mention her. She's *on* the list."

"Jennifer?"

"Embezzlement. She worked at a bank once. She paid it back and they hushed everything up."

I shook my head in astonishment. "What have we

got in this damn company, anyway? The Joliet prison alumni association?"

"Well," said Mike, somewhat wearily, "it's a rare citizen who doesn't bump heads with the law somewhere along the line. How about a couple of our big stars? There's at least one D.W.I. everybody knows about. Technically, drunk-driving's a jail offense, though it usually gets suspended the first time. Anyway, none of these I've mentioned so far are crimes of violence. But we've got one of those, too."

"Don't tell me."

Mike continued anyway. "Sam Rubicoff, our stunt coordinator. He's big, and husky, and a little mean-eyed, so his record didn't surprise me, either. Seems he once belonged to a motorcycle gang. They had a big fight, with sprocket chains or whatever they use. Sam went up for assault. I'm sure he's reformed now, but he *is* one of those who fits into the time and place requirement."

"Let's see, now," I said, still holding the same frown. "What does all this tell us? Not much, as far as I can see. Just that there are a lot of closets around with skeletons in them. And I suppose the implication is that anybody—even somebody we know pretty well and think of as highly innocent—could secretly be involved in this terrible mess. But I think we've admitted that possibility to ourselves all along."

"Look," said Mike, "I didn't guarantee putting all these files together would close the case. It's just the way I do it; motions I have to go through. If nothing else, it starts the wheels spinning. The answer may be somewhere else—outside of the company, for example. We don't have much yet on Trish's boyfriend, Mendoza y Villasenor. Or Luis, the bullfighter, for that matter. Both of whom were in L.A. when Spitalny got it."

"You left somebody out," said Meredy, from the desk.

Mike looked at her. "Yeah? Who?"

"Me. I've got a yellow sheet. And I *could* have been in L.A."

Mike sighed. "You said it. I didn't."

"I've got a bad taste in my mouth," I said. "All this suspicion. And you haven't even considered motive. Why would anybody you've mentioned so far want to commit a string of murders? Or one of the murders, for that matter?"

"We've already kicked that around," said Mike. "The motive's got to be irrational. Except, of course, to the killer—a nut, of course, who's blown his cork."

"Or her cork," said Meredy, shrugging.

"Yeah," said Mike. "Whatever."

I eyed Mike evenly. "Know what all this adds up to? With all the trouble you've taken, you're nowhere—absolutely nowhere."

"You're right," he answered calmly. "But I've been there before."

As always, I checked the bulletin board before we rode out to the set the next morning. It was one of Phyllis Upton's administrative devices, and was used, in addition to the daily call sheet, to keep the company informed. It might contain anything from notations concerning equipment repair for the technical personnel, to personal messages that for one reason or another had not been delivered. Because we occupied the entire hotel, with a spill-over into several nearby *casas de huéspides*, or guest houses, the management didn't mind having this big cork board in the lobby, which had become a kind of center of operations.

In truth, few of the cast or crew paid much attention to this bulletin board, which was tolerated as one of Phyllis's notions. It didn't do any harm, after all. Anything new usually appeared, thumbtacked upon it, in the morning, and that was when nobody was in a mood to pay much attention to anything. For some reason, the task of posting the bulletin board had fallen to Jennifer Schwartz, who was good at taking care of little details nobody else wanted to mess with.

There was a phone message for Mike on the board

this morning. It was on one of these little printed forms that showed the date and time and the name of the person who called. We'd had things like this in the Army, where I'd had to learn to use them, and I can remember how their very efficiency used to irritate me. There is something about forms that says they exist so idiots won't forget details, and this, in turn, implies that you and everyone else around you is an idiot.

I squinted at the message, which said that Luis Mondragon had called and bore the added notation: "Says he remembers name of person outside Blue Pigeon, please get in touch ASAP." I looked around for Mike to call this to his attention, learned that he'd already left for the set in one of the sedans, and made a mental note to tell him about it later, when I saw him.

In the ensuing shuffle I found myself riding out to the set with Jennifer Schwartz. Although most of my mind was on the pages of script I would try to shoot that day, I asked her about the note.

"Oh, that," she said. "Well, this person called the hotel, and they connected him with me instead of Mike. That's Phyllis's idea, so the actors won't be bothered with a lot of unnecessary calls. You'd be surprised at some we get, from all over the country. Fans, mostly, or somebody trying to sell something. The same here as when we're back in Hollywood. So I ask them their business, and if it seems legitimate I connect them."

"But you didn't connect this guy with Mike?"

"At Mike's request. He said he didn't want to be bothered last night by anything. 'Not if Jesus Christ himself calls,' he said. What's he up to, anyway? Something to do with all these murders, I'll bet."

"Better ask Mike himself," I said. "Anyway, I'll pass this on to Mike when I see him."

"Was it important? Who is Luis Mondragon? The name seems vaguely familiar."

"He's just some bullfighter," I said, showing a shrug. "Mike'll take care of it. Forget it."

Telling Jennifer to forget a scrap of gossip was like

telling some Doberman Pinscher not to gobble up a pork chop dropped from the table. "Bullfighter?" She brightened. "I know who it is! It's that boyfriend Wally Demarest was fooling around with!"

"Whoever," I said. "Whatever. His business. Their business. Mike's business. Shall we talk about the weather or something?"

"There's nothing you can say about the weather here. It's always the same. But I've got some other news for you. We're getting another visitation from Peter Revelstoke."

"A visitation, huh?" I reflected to myself that unconsciously she'd put her finger on it. When Revelstoke came to see you it was never a just plain visit. "What's he want this time—a chance to gloat?"

"According to Ira," said Jennifer, "he's going to do an in-depth story on the murders. Ira doesn't like it, but what can he do?"

I sighed. "What can any of us do? Everybody's against us. If that be paranoia, make the most of it. . . ."

During the siesta hour, when the sun was glaring down relentlessly at the yellow dust and glittering adobe walls of the town, Luis Mondragon, professionally known as *El Alacrán*, drove his TR-7 sports car to Meredy Ames's little house.

This is how both Mike and I reconstruct it, anyway. We weren't there. Nobody but Luis and the person he was to meet in a moment were there.

He stepped from the automobile, retrieved a suitcase containing his bullfighting costume from the luggage compartment, and also his *estoque*, or sword. Its curved tip for going in between the bull's shoulder blades was wrapped in velvet. Then he strode, in his lithe and languid way, to the front door of the house.

There is much we merely assume. We know that Meredy was not there because she was on duty in the bar at the Blue Pigeon. From this, we can safely say that Meredy did not send him a message asking him to come to her studio to pose again. But we can be almost sure someone sent him such a message. A phone call would have done it. "Meredy asked me to tell you she'd like you to be there, if you don't mind." Something like that.

He came to the door and found it open. He went inside. It was cooler inside and, since the curtains were drawn, a little darker.

From this point on, we do not know precisely how it was done. Did the person on hand actually greet him and talk to him briefly? Was it someone he knew? Did this person say that Meredy would be along presently, and that he was to make himself comfortable and wait?

Or was there a struggle of some kind?

There were no signs of such a struggle. The room was in perfect order later that afternoon when Meredy returned and found Luis still there.

She found him face down on the floor in an immense pool of blood, with the *estoque* upright and sunken deeply into one of his kidneys.

CHAPTER THIRTEEN

Originally, only Peter Revelstoke, rake in hand (the one for muck), was to have come to Chirapulco. But with the discovery of Luis Mondragon's body, slain by his own sword, journalists from all over were suddenly descending upon us. Quite a few were from the Mexican press and electronic media; *El Alacrán* was achieving, in death, a fame that had eluded him in life. Some were from the entertainment news media, like the feature writer from *TV Guide;* others were from the regular news outlets. The Associated Press had a man there, as did all three major networks. There was even a guy from the huge Mainichi outfit in Japan, covering for their cartel of newspapers and TV stations.

The press corps numbered eighteen, altogether. Ira Yoder was hopping about frantically to keep them reasonably happy and as much out of our hair as possible.

It was hardly fortunate that Luis—not a bad guy at all—had been killed, but, as far as the production was concerned, it was better than the violent death of another member of the company. I think if there had been another murder in our ranks everybody would have quit, then and there, maybe including myself.

Luis's death just didn't seem part of the pattern— though both Mike and I suspected it was. At any rate, Phyllis Upton gave no sign of halting production, and everybody went along with her, though there were numerous scowls and dark, furtive mutterings.

As the members of the press corps watched—and as I tried to forget their presence—I put Blossom Foster and Alex Keglmeyer through their farewell scene at the railroad station—a part of the set that hadn't been demolished by the wild-steer ride through the town. It wasn't a difficult scene to block out, but we had to do more than the usual number of rehearsals and takes on account of both Blossom and Alex lacking experience. I also called for extra camera angles in the hope that the film editor might be able to make the kids look a little better than they actually were. The media types seemed to enjoy it, though they obviously got a little bored between takes when all the necessary details were being set up again.

"Okay—cut!" I said at last. I walked forward to where Blossom and Alex had just finished going through the scene for what must have been the eighth time. "That was nice, kids," I said, "and it's a print. Let's take a break."

Mike and I took the break in Phyllis's administrative trailer, which was air-conditioned. This wasn't our idea; it was Phyllis's. She and Ira Yoder had scheduled an interview between us and Peter Revelstoke, who had specifically asked for it. If he'd asked for the moon she'd have reached up and tried to get that for him, too. Such is the clout that bastards like Revelstoke wield.

The air-conditioning purred in the background. The three of us sat there, amidst Phyllis's office equipment, and sipped cold drinks. Mike and I had canned root beer that had been smuggled in, and Revelstoke had a vodka and tonic brought to the set in spite of Phyllis's no-alcohol rule. Phyllis and Ira had both asked to be present during the interview but Revelstoke, with a lordly gesture, had vetoed that.

He was wearing his safari costume again. That must have been part of the reason for his visit—an excuse to wear it and look dashing. I studied him and wondered again at the phenomenon of Peter Revelstoke. Everybody hated him—even his fans, I think—but everybody tuned into him and hung upon his words. His Nielsen was higher than it was for either of the stupid sit-coms that opposed him on the other two networks during his broadcast time. They changed programs every season in the effort to dislodge him, but never managed to cut him by so much as a point. As a consequence, he made a hell of a lot of money and was permitted to say anything he wished, though some of it made the network execs tremble and grow little ulcers on their big ones.

Mike and I were still sweating from the heat outside but Revelstoke was as dry as baby powder. He held his nose high, over his long upper lip, as though he didn't want it too close to a couple of peons like ourselves.

"Now, then," he said, "about this latest murder. Luis Mondragon was an outsider, but I'm convinced his demise was another in the same series. You probably hoped it wouldn't be noticed. Fortunately, I have informants everywhere, and when it was brought to my attention that Luis was killed in the studio of Miss Meredy Ames, who seems to be a close friend of yours, Michael, I saw a connection immediately and, after some further inquiry, learned that Luis and one of the previous victims, Wally Demarest, had been lovers. I mention all this so you'll be sure to understand that you can no longer sweep this terrible mess under the rug and out of sight. The public is concerned with these murders now, and so am I."

"Okay," I said. "There's been another murder. And we think it may have some connection with the others, too. What else do you want from us?"

"First," said Revelstoke, "I want to know everything Michael has uncovered so far in his investigation. That should be good for at least one column filled with exclusive revelations."

Mike shook his head. "I've got nothing to give you. I'm up against a stone wall, same as everybody else."

"Come on now, Michael," Revelstoke said. "I know you've been going at it hammer and tongs. I know that our steadfast captain of detectives, Alfonso Cruz, has warned you to keep your grubby little fingers out of it. But I know that you've been working on it nevertheless, and it's safe to say, I think, that you're holding out on Cruz. Do not hold out on me. If I feel you're not cooperating, I can do more damage than Cruz ever thought of doing."

"How many times do I have to say it?" said Mike, making like a bulldog with his lower jaw. "There's nothing to hold out."

"Is it possible," said Revelstoke, languidly shifting his position in his chair, "is it by any chance possible that you already *know* who the murderer is and won't reveal it because of what it might do to the picture? Is it someone prominent? One of your overpaid and over-worshiped stars, perhaps?"

"I dare you to say something like that on the air or in print," said Mike. "I'll sue your ass off."

Revelstoke laughed. "My dear Michael, you're talking to an expert. I know how to say things and remain unsueable."

I couldn't remain silent any longer. "Okay, you guys," I said, "this is getting off on the wrong foot again. Can we all act like civilized adults for a change? Let me review the bidding here—maybe that'll calm things down. To begin, look at our side of it, Peter. Forget whatever you think of *The Godless* artistically; it's a job we're doing and it's a job we all need to do, in some cases for sheer survival. Along the way, we've got to do a lot of things we'd rather not—like sucking up to you. Phyllis gave me strict instructions to cooperate and, to the point it makes me throw up, that's what I intend to do. If you'll ask answerable questions, Peter, and keep the personal barbs out of it, we'll do our best to answer them. What more do you want?"

"I've already told you the first thing I want. All of Michael's information. The second is your promise that when and if he discovers the identity of the murderer, I get the story before anybody else does."

"In a pig's ass," growled Mike.

"No, wait." I waved Mike down. "We just might be able to do something like that, Peter. But it would have to be a trade."

"For what?" He looked a little suspicious.

"Let me explain what Mike's been doing, so you'll see what I mean. As he likes to say, murder cases in real life are solved by very mundane means. By informers, file cabinets, computer printouts. What it adds up to is information. About the victims and suspects and all the people connected with them. Tons of information that is sorted through patiently until, maybe, if he's lucky, the investigator begins to see a pattern. Am I getting this right, Mike?"

He shrugged. "That's about it."

"Well, within the limits of what's available to him, Mike's been doing that, here in Chirapulco. We were able to get the police records on a few people that had them. Those you can't have, by the way; making them public might do a great deal of harm. But there's another kind of information that you might be able to give *us*. Scandal, gossip, whatever you want to call it. The kind of juicy bits our own Jennifer Schwartz likes to collect and share so generously with anyone in earshot. The kind you must always be collecting to feed your column with. Who is sleeping with whom. What erstwhile happy couple is taking a trip to Splitsville. Who beats their dogs or secretly belongs to the Ku Klux Klan. You know the kind of thing I mean. Ordinarily, we'd shut our ears to it, but this time it might help fill in the picture." I turned to Mike. "Would you be agreeable to such a trade?"

"I don't know," said Mike, scowling deeply.

"I don't know, either," said Revelstoke. "Can you be more specific about what you want?"

"Simple," I said. "We reel off a few names. As you hear each one, you tell us what you know in the way of scandal. We keep it confidential, of course, and the only way any of it will ever get out is if the murders are solved, and the information has to be exposed as evidence. Let's understand one thing about this deal, however. What we hear may not enable Mike to get a line on the murderer. In which case, we don't owe you a thing."

"But if anything I provide does lead to a solution,

then I'm to be advised of the murderer's identity twenty-four hours before anyone else?"

"That's too long. Make it four hours."

"Twelve?"

"Okay, twelve. Is that all right with you, Mike?"

"What am I getting into?" Mike groaned.

"Let's find out," I said. "Come on, Mike. You go down the list, and let's hear what Peter has to say."

He looked at me sourly for a minute, then said, "Okay. There are several people who could have committed the murders when it comes to time and place. Let's cover them all—even the ones that seem impossible."

"Right," I said. "Way to go."

"George Kennedy," he said.

"What?" I glared at him.

Mike was deadpan. "You said *everybody*. That includes you, too, George. You're without an alibi for every murder except the bullfighter's, and we can't say for sure that one belongs to the others. Nothing personal, George. I'm just being thorough—like a good cop should."

"A little too damn thorough, if you ask me," I said, glowering.

Revelstoke showed a restrained smile—his way of laughing uproariously, I think. "Well, George, you invented the rules of this game, don't you know, so I think you'll have to stick with them. Let me see, what do I know about you that's scandalous? Not a great deal, I'm afraid. You probably spend too much money on that airplane of yours and this probably leads to bitter quarrels at home—"

"It doesn't," I said, feeling my neck get hot, "and if it did, it wouldn't be any of your goddamn business."

"My dear George," said Revelstoke, "the moment your name—or anybody's name—is included in the credits of one of those mindless films Hollywood grinds out in such profusion and foists upon a hapless public, it *is* my business."

"In that case," I said, "we include Mike himself."

"Me?" Now it was Mike's turn to glare.

"Quite," said Revelstoke. "Nothing on you lately, Michael, I'm happy to say. There was that so-called starlet you took to Las Vegas for a weekend just before your divorce, of course—"

"How the hell did you know about that?"

"Pure omniscience," said Revelstoke. "But let's continue with the list."

"Okay," said Mike, calming down a little and furrowing his brow as he shuffled names in his head. "How about Phyllis Upton?"

Revelstoke shrugged. "Scandal-free, for the most part. Not very beautiful—as we all know—but exceptionally bright. She belongs to that absurd high-IQ society, Mensa. They have meetings and keep asking each other 'if you're so smart, why ain't you rich?' which few of them seem to be. Maybe that's what gave her a near nervous breakdown a few years ago and drove her to a shrink. I'd have one, too, if I had to put up with the idiots that make up the cast of practically any motion picture—"

"Would it drive you to murder?" Mike was deadpan.

"It might, at that," drawled Revelstoke. "But I haven't succumbed to that natural temptation to commit a massacre, if that's what you're thinking. Continue, Michael. Who's next?"

"Dean Martin?"

"A clown," said Revelstoke, shrugging.

"Hardly," I said, springing loyally to Dean's defense. "He's done some damn good straight dramatic roles—and wait till you see his performance in *The Godless.*"

"I doubt," said Revelstoke airily, "if any of us will ever have the opportunity to witness any of the performances in *The Godless.* Look, Michael, forget the big stars. You can rule them out before we begin, because they're all really too stupid to commit a series of rather clever murders."

"Look, Revelstoke," said Mike, tapping a stubby

finger on the desk top, "let me decide who I want to consider as suspects, okay?"

"Hey, guys," I said, interrupting, "calm down, okay? This exercise isn't gonna work if you two keep making a dogfight out of it. Calmly now, Mike. Who's the next one on your list?"

"Well, let's see. We've already got several with police records of one sort or another."

"Have you considered Blossom Foster?" Revelstoke asked blandly.

"No," said Mike. "Why? Has she got a police record?"

"No police record—but you know how she really got her part in this picture, don't you?"

"We know it's not like Ira Yoder says in his publicity releases," I said. "Lance Haverford didn't find her in a burger joint; she walked in and applied for work on a regular casting call."

"I've no doubt they went through the motions of a casting call," said Revelstoke. "But Lance Haverford— rest his soul and all that—was an absolute satyr. I don't believe this is news to you; everyone in the industry knew it. The statutory rape episode was the only time this little peccadillo of his received widespread public notice. In point of fact, Lance Haverford would go to bed with anything female—and I do mean *anything*. Among several hundred others, he got to Blossom Foster. Rendered her pregnant. Much to Cora Foster's delight. After the abortion, she blackmailed Lance into giving Blossom the role."

"Are you sure?" said Mike, glaring sourly at Revelstoke. "How come you never dropped this juicy bit in one of your shows?"

"I've been saving it," said Revelstoke, "against the rare chance that *The Godless* ever comes to the screen."

Mike looked at me. "If this is true, it's the first thing in the way of a motive we've found for any of the murders. Cora *might* have harbored a grudge against Lance.

But she'd have no reason I can see to knock off all those other people."

"And that," said Revelstoke, "is what you arrive at, inevitably, when any of your so-called suspects are considered. Logically, you are left with only two possible answers. One—the murders are separate, committed by more than one person with more than one motive. Two, there is no clear-cut motive and the murders are therefore the work of a raving lunatic."

"Or, three," said Mike, a little slowly and grimly, "the motive's so far out it's one that just hasn't occurred to us before."

"What do you mean by that?"

"Well, the killer could be a nut, in the sense that his motive is weird—one that wouldn't be a motive to most of us. But let's say there's someone who hates *The Godless* so much he's willing to murder a bunch of people just to keep it from ever getting finished. That would fit *you*, Revelstoke, wouldn't it?"

"Absurd!" said Revelstoke, drawing himself up.

"Yeah," said Mike. "But no more absurd than everything else we've thought about."

The sky was clear in every direction from the Chirapulco airport. Clear and turquoise blue, with the hot sun hanging in the sky. It shouldn't have been absolutely clear, because at least one speck should have been in it—the approaching daily commercial flight from what we had all begun to call the outside world. But there was no speck, because the daily plane was late again.

I stood in the small terminal building with Phyllis Upton as we both looked out over the flat landing field and the rolling desert earth that stretched out beyond it, resembling a rumpled chenille bedspread. Phyllis, with a sure instinct for what would make her even more unattractive, was wearing some kind of bare-armed top and a Madras skirt of bright and motley patches.

She stared into the distance. "I wonder what Fargo's bringing us. A reprieve—or a warrant for our execution?

The plane would be late. I don't know how much longer I can stand waiting."

"He must have given you some hint of why he's coming here."

Phyllis shook her head. "Not a word. Just that he and the missus were on their way. Hold everything, he said, till they got here."

"Does he have any idea what it costs to hold everything? We were supposed to be shooting this morning— now the schedule's all screwed up again."

"I tried to explain," said Phyllis, "but I don't think he was listening. George, do you realize where we are now, budget-wise? I went over it with the accountant this morning. We have not only used up every cent of the funds allotted to us, but we're overdrawn by several thousand. That's got to come out of my own pocket before the next round of paychecks will be honored."

I frowned. "Somebody'll cover it. A few thousand's a drop in the bucket. We can't let the whole picture die for what, in this case, amounts to loose change."

"You'd think so, wouldn't you? But the way it's set up, Fargo countersigns all fund transfers, and if he doesn't cover it, either with his own money or somebody else's, we're sunk. Even if he does cover it, we may be sunk. We haven't got anything left for post-production. Editing, music, titles, studio retakes, opticals—they've all got to be as first-class as the rest of the picture or we haven't got anything but a mishmash of footage. Add to that the publicity and advertising we still need, and we're looking at another million—maybe two million."

"That sounds like a lot," I said, "but it's actually not excessive. Other pictures have gone over that much before, and found the extra money somewhere."

"In past years, maybe," said Phyllis. "But with money as tight as it is now, nobody's going to put seven figures into what amounts to a wild speculation. And *The Godless* is that, not a sound investment. Even its bankable stars and the publicity it's already had don't guarantee a big box office. First, it's a western. Nobody's made a western since the golden days; audiences just don't come to see them anymore, though nobody knows why. It was a gamble right from the beginning that *The Godless*, through its sheer excellence, could surmount that obstacle. Second, our publicity's been the wrong kind. Don't ask me how it happened—I certainly didn't foresee it—but somehow the murders made all the hype Ira's been grinding out backfire. You know what I'd do if I were an investor? I'd corner the market on ten-foot poles. People are going to be wanting them to avoid touching *The Godless*."

I shook my head stubbornly. "You keep expecting the worst, Phyllis. You'll push it through somehow. We were all knocked silly by Lance's murder, of course, but, aside from that, we were glad to see you take over. We've got more confidence in you than you have in yourself."

"That's nice to hear," said Phyllis, sighing deeply, "but I don't know if it really helps. I keep feeling that Lance would have been lucky—that he'd have found some miracle to save everything at the last moment. But everything *I* touch turns to dreck. It's been that way ever since I was born. . . ."

The arriving airplane appeared in the sky at last. Phyllis and I stepped forward to go out on the ramp and meet J. Sutton Fargo. He smiled when he saw me, and Marilou waved. A moment later she was kissing me wetly and calling me "Jo-werdge." We went through the amenities, which consisted of intoducing Phyllis—with whom he'd talked on the phone but had never met—and arranging for him to pick up his luggage.

It was all small talk as we rode from the airport to the hotel in a sedan, but the air was full of tight electricity, as both Phyllis and Fargo waited for the right moment to get down to cases. Marilou provided most of the conversation as she gushed about how thrilled she was to actually be on location and see all of her favorite stars in performance before the cameras. I then came up with an idea I still think was a stroke of genius.

"Marilou," I said, "we're working on a scene right

now where there's a crowd of townfolk in the background. How would you like to put on a costume and be an extra?"

"Why, Jo-werdge! You mean, *be* in a movie? I'd love it!"

Fargo said, "That's nice," and frowned privately.

Phyllis and I glanced at each other. She tumbled right away to what I was doing. I was making it possible for us to shoot at least one more scene. Fargo wouldn't deny his wife a lousy ten thousand or so for an opportunity like this.

We were in the streets of the town and almost to the hotel before Phyllis found just the right pause for inserting what was really on our minds.

"I suppose you've come here, Mr. Fargo, just to get a good look at how we do it—is that it?"

"That's part of it, Miss Upton. Phyllis? I'll call you Phyllis, and you call me Sut, okay? I've come here to make up my mind. Let me spell it out for you, so nobody gets any wrong ideas. Open and aboveboard—that's the way I do business."

"So I've heard," said Phyllis. "And that's what I prefer, too."

Fargo, against the heat, was wearing a loose sports shirt that exposed the reddish fuzz of hair on his tanned and muscular forearms. In this costume he did not look any more like an oil tycoon than he had in his well-tailored, eastern-style suits back in L.A. I mention this as a kind of rebuke to myself, because I have a way of stereotyping people according to the way they'd be cast in movies, in which a Texas mogul like Fargo would always be big and bumptious instead of small, quiet, and just a little sinister. You could see that behind his polite and placid facade, the wheels were always turning.

"When I heard about this bullfighter being murdered," said Fargo, "and the way he and that stunt man of yours had been carryin' on homosexually, that just about ripped it. We got an old poem back home that pretty much says how I feel about it. Maybe you heard it. 'Two things I can't understand, is a bull-dykin' woman and a pansy man.' These days you're supposed to understand 'em and, as far as I can figure it out, even fall all over yourself to give 'em employment, the way you have to do with minorities. You know who the minorities really are now? They're the plain old white Anglo-Saxon Protestants, like you and me. When are *we* gonna get a break, for a change?"

"Sut," said Marilou, "you're getting yourself all stirred up again."

"Yes. Well, as George here knows, I've been on the edge of droppin' this whole project for some time. I didn't go into it in the first place for strictly money-makin' reasons—I figured I'd do some good by promotin' certain ideals I believe we've got to readopt before we crash, just like the Roman Empire did when it lost its moral fiber. Frankly, it hasn't worked out that way. These murders have turned it all around. It's just like this fella, Revelstoke, says—though he looks to me like another fag—they're symbolic of what's really behind this whole effort."

"I think we understand how you feel," Phyllis said cautiously. "Did you come all this way just to tell us?"

"I came because Marilou coaxed me. One last look before you decide, she said. That was a fair piece of advice, whether she knew it or not. If one of my companies is about to go belly up, I always take one last look before I let it sink."

"Then we still might be able to finish the picture?"

"We'll see," said Fargo, his frown deepening.

I tried to concentrate on the continued shooting that afternoon as Phyllis and Ira Yoder took the Fargos in tow and gave them a two-dollar tour of Chirapulco and the location area. In my last glance at Phyllis there was a plea to keep them out of my hair as much as she could, and I think she understood it. Marilou, as I heard later, was thrilled to be socializing with Glenn Ford and Dean Martin, both of whom had been tipped off by Phyllis so that they turned on the charm for Marilou and Fargo; though, skillful performers that they were, they didn't lay it on too thick. Fargo himself must have been on his best behavior, because he refrained from rubbing Glenn and Dean the wrong way with any of his jingoistic observations, and I'm sure they never even realized that in his heart he was six degrees to the right of John Birch and Benito Mussolini. Hell, he himself didn't realize that.

Some of the media reporters, who were still with us, hung around the set and watched the shooting. Whenever I glanced at them I was struck with the irony of it. Here we had a million dollars worth of free publicity—the kind you can't buy—for a picture that might never be shown.

That night there was the usual gathering in the hotel cantina. I didn't join in; I ordered dinner sent up to my room and, as I waited for it, took a long shower, staying in it until the hot water began to turn cold.

As I came back into the room with a towel around my middle, I heard a knock on the door and opened it to find Mike Corby, instead of the waiter with a tray I'd expected.

"George," he said, "I gotta talk to you."

"I'm waiting for dinner. You want to order something?"

He shook his head and sat on the edge of the sofa as I changed into a jogging suit. I don't use jogging suits for jogging, which is the most boring form of exercise I know, but for lounging around in, which I'd rather do any day. Mike said, "You know that journal Phyllis keeps?"

"What journal?"

"In her trailer. You must have seen it. Journal, record, whatever you want to call it. One of her administrative devices. A log—like a desk sergeant keeps in a police station. What civilians always call a 'blotter,' though I don't know why."

"Oh. That one." I dimly recalled Phyllis making an

172

entry in the ledgerlike book the last time I'd seen her in her sanctuary.

"Little notes about everybody and everything that comes in or goes out," Mike continued. "It's one reason, I guess, she's so efficient and always knows what's going on. Now, as you know, I've been trying to put this murder thing together, and places and times are an important part of it. I suddenly realized that a lot of it was already laid out for me, right there in Phyllis's journal. She was busy entertaining all our visitors, and I didn't have time to find her and ask her for it. So I went into the trailer and took a good look at it, anyway."

"She keeps the trailer locked," I said, my eye on Mike.

"That must have been why it was so hard to get in," he said, grinning.

"Back to your old habits, I see."

"Well, they paid off this time. I went over the damn thing carefully, and after a while I was able to figure out Phyllis's abbreviations, which amount to a kind of shorthand. Never mind the details, but what I could see was where just about anybody in the company was at any given time on any day since we started shooting here. Meredy and I, putting those files together, have already set up a chronological table in that respect, but we've been concentrating on the suspects. But what about the victims themselves?"

"Well, what about them?"

"Back home," said Mike, getting a wistful gleam in his eye, "in the old days, when I had an office, and files, and third-grade detectives to do my legwork for me, I would always compile dossiers on the victims of any murder case. You can see how a victim's recent activities and known associates might lead you to whoever killed him—it's S.O.P. in any investigation. But out here in the boondocks I just didn't have the time and facilities to include that, so I kind of let it slide. I shouldn't have. Because, in going over Phyllis's log, I found a pattern— a lead. It looks like the best one yet."

The waiter arrived with my supper and I went through the routine of accepting it and fishing in my trousers for pesos to tip him with, overtipping as usual because I couldn't figure out the exchange rate in my head fast enough. When he had gone, and when I had begun to eat, Mike continued.

"What did most of the victims have in common?" said Mike.

"Getting killed?" I asked, deadpan.

"You know what I mean. A pattern. Something they were all involved in. I'll tell you what it was. They were all having love affairs. Trish Wainwright with that *hidalgo* of hers. Wally Demarest and his bullfighter. Lance Haverford with person or persons unknown. It's an assumption in his case, but a pretty strong one; with that sex drive of his you can bet he wasn't letting his libido go ungratified. The only difference is that he managed to be more discreet about it than anybody else, so we don't know yet precisely who was keeping him happy in his spare time. The next victim, Nick Spitalny, doesn't fit the list because his murder was probably a cover-up, to keep us from learning who procured a silencer from him. Let's move on to Joel Totterelli. He was a very quiet guy, and nobody ever noticed, but he had himself a little playmate, too. Jennifer Schwartz."

"Jenny? The original puritan?"

"I know," said Mike, "I sound like I'm spreading rumors now, the way she always does, but she's young and healthy and not too bad looking, especially in the bazoom department, so she's entitled to a sex life, the same as anybody else. I know about Jennifer and Joel because I asked her."

"And she *admitted* it?"

"She didn't have to. The way she blushed and got furious over the question was enough."

"Mike," I said, crunching a taco, which dribbled out of the sides and all over my fingers, the way tacos do, "I'm getting lost here. What did Phyllis's journal have to do with you suddenly deciding that people were pairing off this way?"

"It *showed* them pairing off on several occasions. That's on account of the old monastery."

"What's that got to do with it?"

"Look," said Mike. "Back in L.A. or someplace, if anyone wanted a roll in the hay they'd go to something like a motel. Nothing like that around here. This hotel's no good for it because there's too much chance of being seen. The little *casas de huéspides* in town don't take one-night stands. But the old monastery, with all its little rooms, and even running spring water, is ideal. You'll remember several people camped out there when we were shooting in that location. And they have those squatter families that live there all the time. Besides, it's just over the hill—maybe an hour's drive. Well, the people who went there checked out cars and of course had to log them out. The log makes its way to Phyllis's office, where she keeps track of all such details. She also wants to know where she can reach anybody in off-duty hours and instituted that sign-out system everybody grumbles about. The upshot is that there's a record, though in fairness to Phyllis, I have to say I don't think she kept it for prying into private lives, and possibly didn't even see what I see in it."

"I still don't understand what you think you see. Trish, Wally, Lance, Joel, all slipping away for a little R and R. So what? We've all done that, or something like it in our time. Even you, according to Revelstoke."

"But it's a pattern," he said doggedly. "The only one we've got. Look—make a list of the victims. The true victims, you might say. We've had eight deaths, but four of them don't fit as what we might call basic murders— *original, intended* victims—see what I mean? Ferdy Holtz and Roberta Vale died as the result of an accident, as unforeseen by the murderer as it was by everybody else. If that plane crash had occurred without the other deaths we'd have taken it in stride as one of those terrible things that happen sometimes—which is exactly what it was.

Spitalny, the arms dealer, and Luis, the bullfighter, were murdered, to be sure, but as a consequence of the other murders. Each of them had to be killed before he talked and pointed a finger toward the murderer. So it's the four originals who supply our pattern. And the pattern is this: *all the victims were having love trysts.*"

"Okay—call it a pattern. But it still doesn't lead us anywhere."

"Maybe it does. At least it opens up another question. We have to ask ourselves that question now. Who's against love trysts? So much against them they're willing to punish them with murder? It calls for a real flake to think that way, but we've already decided that's what our murderer is."

"If that's the motive," I said thoughtfully, "what about you and Meredy? You two have been playing house. That makes you eligible as the next victims."

Mike nodded. "I've already thought of that. And it's part of what I want to do next."

"What's that?"

"Set a trap. If the murderer thinks I'm getting close, and if I fit his requirements as a victim, anyway, he might make a play. Then I zero in on him."

"Or he does the zeroing before you have a chance. Anyway, how do you set this trap?"

"A press conference," said Mike. "Get all the reporters together and tell 'em I'm working on a strong lead, and that the killer will be identified very shortly. It's an old technique. Cops do it all the time when they haven't really got anything. It makes the perpetrator nervous as hell and much more likely to give himself away. What I want you to do, George, is ask Phyllis to set it up."

"Why don't you ask her yourself?"

"Because it might get back to the killer that the suggestion came from me, and he might see through the trap. He's probably got a first-class mind, remember, even if it is twisted. Also, if Phyllis knows the idea's mine—and why—that might get out, too. One hint of it to somebody like Jennifer Schwartz and it's all over the place."

"This is screwy," I said. I could feel my own frown squinching my face down into a nest of wrinkles.

"Yeah," said Mike blandly. "You gonna do it for me?"

I pushed away the half-finished plate of tacos, tamales, and refried beans, which, here in the land of their origin, seemed not as tasty as in some fast-food joint back in L.A.; and after looking at Mike for a long moment, I nodded and said, "Yeah."

CHAPTER FOURTEEN

The press conference was called in the same banquet room where Phyllis had assembled the company after Lance's death to announce that she was taking over as producer. Not all the company was present this time; only the major actors, some of the administrative personnel, and those of the technical staff who weren't needed out at the set to make everything ready for the last few scenes.

The reporters were there in full force. They'd been about to leave, but had cancelled their flights out when Phyllis had advised them that Mike Corby would reveal certain new developments concerning the murders. Peter Revelstoke sat in the center of the front row, looking haughty and doubtful.

J. Sutton and Marilou Fargo sat together a few seats back. She had a stenographer's notebook in her lap, a pencil poised over it. She'd decided to try her hand at writing a piece for her local paper back home about her visit to the location where a genuine motion picture was being filmed. They'd probably print it. Her husband owned about half of the newspaper, anyway.

I had used the Fargos' presence as leverage in persuading Phyllis to hold the press conference. She'd been reluctant, at first, when I approached her with the idea, saying I'd learned Mike had made some progress in his investigation, and that I thought sharing this with the media might generate some favorable publicity for us, for a change. Even better, I added, was that it might give Fargo a more favorable impression of us—might even help him to change his mind about dropping the whole project. "Let him see we're all straight arrows and not morally depraved, as he thinks, and that we take care of our own dirty laundry."

Phyllis wondered just how much Mike had really discovered. "If he hasn't got anything substantial, it could backfire," she said. "Revelstoke will call it more Hollywood hype. So will the other reporters, this time." I had to admit I didn't know what Mike had in the way of hard facts, and I thought for a moment I'd lost the skirmish, until Ira Yoder got into it, and, hopping about like a sparrow in the wake of a cavalry troop, told Phyllis he thought a press conference was a great idea and she'd better be sure to have free drinks and lots of canapés.

So here we were, and there was Phyllis, up on the little dais and behind the lectern, opening the proceedings. She had a good voice and a commanding presence; it almost made you forget that she looked like something created by special effects for some drive-in movie about a creature from the swamp. She recapped the murders briefly, summed up Mike's background as a cop before he became an actor, and then said that he had an important announcement. "Ladies and gentlemen . . . Mike Corby."

Mike ran his eyes over the audience as though he intended to put a make on the culprit then and there. "I guess you all know by now that I've been taking a look into these apparent homicides out here on location. One thing you must have noticed about them is that all have different M.O.'s—a knifing, a poisoning, a shooting, and so on. Ordinarily, this would suggest different killers, and that in itself would be weird: why would a bunch of killers suddenly decide to knock off a series of victims in a certain place and in a very short span of time? It's easier to believe one killer, and when we work on that hypothesis we begin to form a picture of our suspect."

A hand went up. It was the little guy in the dark suit who came either from *Time* or *Newsweek*—I forget which. "Mr. Corby, have you managed to identify the killer?"

"I'll get to that," said Mike. "And save the questions for later, okay?"

Jennifer Schwartz, sitting next to me, leaned my way enough to brush against me with one of her immense, Partonesque mammaries, and said, "Does he really know who it is, George?"

"Search me." I shrugged.

"A single perpetrator," continued Mike, "and one with a warped mind. But that doesn't mean a stupid mind. Some of the murders were ingenious; only a very clever person could have planned them that carefully and carried them out. So that gives us two things to look for. Somebody flaked-out inside, but otherwise bright. This kind of mental disturbance is hard to spot. The subject seems perfectly normal until whatever's bugging the mental and emotional circuits gets triggered off. Psychologists have this well-labeled as a form of paranoia; it seems to hit people who are otherwise sharp, or even brilliant."

Revelstoke, his legs crossed languidly as he lounged in his folding chair, striking his pose of an aristocrat born a hundred years too late, said, "Michael, we didn't come here for an elementary lecture on abnormal psychology, don't you know."

"Let me tell this my way, okay, Pete?"

"As long as you—uh—stick to the rules of the game," said Revelstoke. The others didn't know why he said that, but I did. He was afraid Mike was going to break his agreement to let Revelstoke know the murderer's identity before anyone else did. I was wondering myself if Mike had changed his mind about that.

"Usually, in investigating a homicide," Mike went on, "we look for a motive. But the motive of somebody this twisted is likely to be one we wouldn't understand very well even if we knew what it was. What we get in cases like this is voices whispering in the ear, complicated logic where two and two makes five. Like in all the classic multiple homicides from Jack the Ripper to Son of Sam. What it adds up to is that we can just about disregard motive, and accept the fact that the murders *have* been committed, for reasons that make sense only to the murderer."

This time it was Phyllis, sitting on my other side, who nudged me. "I don't think he knows *anything*, George. He's faking—beating around the bush. Maybe we shouldn't have had this press conference."

"Too late to call it off now," I whispered back.

"Now I haven't got time here," said Mike, continuing, "to trace all the ins and outs of the legwork and paper-shuffling we did to narrow down our list of suspects. But we did arrive at such a list—all those who had an actual opportunity to commit the murders. And then we started eliminating these suspects, one by one, for various reasons. We finally boiled it down to somebody, and that's why I called you all here today."

There was a dead pause as everyone in the room stared back at Mike. A cockroach ran across the floor somewhere, and I think I heard its footsteps.

Revelstoke broke the pause. "Don't tell me you actually *know* who it is!"

"I think I know," said Mike, nodding. "But I still haven't got any hard evidence that would stand up in court. This is a common situation in a murder investigation. Sometimes cops spend more time developing sufficient evidence than they do identifying the perpetrator in the first place."

"Well, for God's sake, who is it?" Revelstoke blurted out.

"I'm afraid, at this point, I can't say," Mike answered calmly.

"Then why, in the name of Jehoshaphat, are you holding this absurd press conference?"

"To give the murderer a chance to confess," said Mike. "You must all be familiar with the psychology of murderers like this one. Deep down, they *want* to be caught. It's a big relief to them when they are. All the terrible pressure off, at last. I can't guarantee that the murderer, hearing what I say, will come forth now, but it's a definite possibility, and I'm gambling on it."

As everyone stirred in his seat, Revelstoke untangled himself from his languid pose and stood up. "Are you saying, Michael, that the murderer is right here in this room—among us at this very moment?"

"I don't think I'd better answer that right now," said Mike.

"That means he is!" Revelstoke turned, and glanced at everyone present. Everyone present was glancing at each other. There were frowns and looks of amazement. Revelstoke faced Mike again. "Either that," he said, "or you're pulling off the most colossal bit of chicanery I have ever witnessed, even in Hollywood, the humbug capital of the world!"

I ran my eyes over the assembled group, twisting in my chair in order to do it. Had this been a scene I was directing, I would have had the camera pan across all the faces at this point, just like that. Which would have been a cliché, right out of Agatha Christie, but, damnit, clichés do happen in real life and that's how they get to be clichés. First, Jennifer Schwartz and Phyllis Upton, on either side of me. Revelstoke himself, standing there and glaring at Mike. In the next row back, Dean Martin, Glenn Ford, Alex Keglmeyer, Blossom Foster, and her mother. Then, Sam Rubicoff, with his pro-wrestler's build and hairy arms. The college-boy production assistant who always faded into the wallpaper, even when there weren't any walls. Beyond them, Meredy Ames, who had slipped in quietly after the conference had begun, and, to my surprise, Ernesto Mendoza y Villasenor, looking as though he owned the place, and maybe he did, at that. And finally, J. Sutton Fargo and Marilou, who still had her stenographer's notebook in her lap, with a pencil poised over it.

The expressions I saw didn't tell me anything. They were all blank. In the movies, characters have to react to startling news, so the audience will know it's startling. In real life, I've noticed, the faces just go blank.

Mike held the pause with perfect timing; he probably had more acting talent than he himself believed. When everybody had looked blank just long enough, he said, "I'm giving this certain party twenty-four hours. All it takes is to come to me and say, 'Mike, I'm the one.' I'll see to it that no one gets hurt and that all rights of the accused are preserved. The Mexican authorities, with the media watching closely, are going to do it all strictly by the book. And tomorrow morning, at this same time, we'll have another press conference. Let's hope that by then I'll be able to give you the perpetrator's name."

I didn't have time to observe the reactions of the various reporters to Mike's announcement. I heard later that they were mixed; that some got to telephones and filed stories on it, and that others, like Revelstoke, decided it was a bluff and just let it go. They all made arrangements to stay at least one more day in Chirapulco, however, so that they could be present at Mike's second press conference. Just in case.

Mike, I noticed, got out of the banquet room fast, before they could gang up on him. I wanted to talk to him, as everybody else did, but the shooting schedule was running late again and I didn't have time. Mike disappeared. I had no idea where to. Meredy's pad, I supposed, where he could relax and be comforted. If I had been Mike, that's where I would have gone.

Heading for the set, I found myself with Phyllis Upton in the sedan, which an incurious Mexican driver took over the bumpy, dusty road with great concentration. What he was concentrating on was not missing a bump.

Phyllis kept stirring in her seat instead of sinking back into it comfortably. "The whole thing was dumb!" she said. "I shouldn't have let you and Ira talk me into it!"

"Well, it seemed a waste of time," I admitted; "but I don't think it did a great deal of harm."

"I'm afraid it did. The other reporters will be like Revelstoke now; convinced we're all a bunch of fumbling idiots, who couldn't possibly make a worthwhile motion picture. What was Mike dreaming of when he stood up there and asked the murderer to walk up to him and make a confession? I don't know a great deal about murderers, but I have a strong feeling they just don't give themselves up that way!"

"That's how it struck me, too," I said, with a little sigh.

"George," she said, "you've been helping Mike in this investigation. Does he really have an idea who the murderer is?"

"He didn't tell me. As for how much he knows, your guess is as good as mine."

"He never should have worked on the case in the first place. But I suppose I'm to blame for that. I thought it would somehow make a good impression on Fargo. Now it's the other way around. Did you see the look on Fargo's face before we left?"

"I didn't notice."

"I could tell what he was thinking. All of us are not only morally depraved but singularly stupid. It tips the scales. Now he *is* going to pull out."

"Unless Mike comes up with the murderer's identity tomorrow," I said.

Phyllis shook her head and frowned. "He won't. He can't possibly. . . ."

It was not easy for me to give all of my attention to the task of directing the rest of the day, and I had to shoot more retakes than I'd intended, which put us even further behind schedule. Although I tried to go back in time a hundred years to the era of the story—something I'd been asking the actors to do—my mind kept wandering back to the sense of disaster that was all around us, here in the present. The irony of our situation was almost too much to bear. Here we had an almost-finished picture, and, I was sure, a very good one. But it was still in the form of numerous reels of exposed film, which had not yet been put together into so much as a rough cut, and this made it virtually unmarketable. All of our efforts—the brilliant sequences Lance Haverford and Joel Totterelli had achieved, the excellent performances most of the actors had given, and my own minor contribution in wrapping up the last few scenes—might never be seen by more than a handful of persons in a screening room, and even then not in final, integrated form.

It was hurting everybody who had put anything—from piggy-bank savings to pieces of their hearts—into the film. More than any other art form, films need both a financial and a creative input in order to come to life. This tends to polarize those who undertake to make them. There are those to whom the film is just another product to be manufactured and distributed for as large a profit margin as possible. And there are those who put their very guts into the effort and get very impatient when financial considerations are so much as mentioned. They're married to each other, and they hate each other, but they need each other if films are to be made at all.

At any rate, I tried to continue on the set as though the production of *The Godless* was not plagued by the slightest trouble. The actors, who knew as much about the tightness of the situation as I did, went along with it and gave the best that was in them. We worked until the director of photography said the waning light would no longer give a color-match to what we'd shot before.

As the caravan of vehicles to take us back to the hotel assembled on the road, I saw a cloud of dust approaching from the town. Before we could begin our own departure, several police-filled jeeps rolled up, with Alfonso Cruz in the lead car, just as he'd been the day he'd interrupted our shooting of Blossom in the pool scene.

I'm big, and I guess that makes me conspicuous. Phyllis was somewhere, though not in sight, and Cruz stepped up to me. He was big enough for his eyes to be level with mine. He leveled them on me like a couple of laser beams.

"I must ask you, Senor Kennedy," he said, "to find Senor Corby for me."

I shook my head. "He's not here, captain. He's not on call today."

"They come here often when they are not on call, no? I was told at the hotel Senor Corby had gone somewhere. Where else would he go but here?"

"You can look around if you want. You won't find him." I glanced at the armed retinue in the jeeps. "What do you want him for, anyway?"

"To arrest him," said Cruz.

"What?"

"I repeat, senor. To arrest him." His expression was a pool of crude oil. "The charge is interfering with a police investigation."

"Hey, come on now," I said. "This whole SWAT team of yours for a minor charge like that?"

"I do not regard it as minor. I warned Senor Corby a number of times, but he continued interfering. What is more, withholding evidence. I have been advised that he held a press conference this morning. That he claims to know the identity of a murderer. Failing to report this to the proper authorities is against the law, senor. And I have lost patience. I have decided to keep Senor Corby in custody where he can no longer interfere."

"Look, never mind all the ins and outs of your law, captain, local or otherwise. I've got an idea you can interpret the law pretty much the way you want out here in the boondocks. But locking Mike Corby up isn't going to do you all that much good. We've only got a couple of days of shooting left, and then he'll be out of here. We all will. Out of your hair forever."

"So I understand. But I will not put up with even one more day of Senor Corby's interference. On the other hand, I am not an unreasonable man, Senor Kennedy. If Senor Corby will agree to leave immediately, I am sure I can arrange to drop the charges and release him."

I frowned. "He can't leave now. I've got one more scene with Mike in it. It's a key scene—can't be left out or the whole story falls apart. We'd have to shoot a lot of the picture all over again, and we don't have the funds for it."

"We all have our problems, Senor Kennedy," said Cruz, fishing for one of his foul cigarettes. "And that one happens to be yours. . . ."

* * *

When I got back to the hotel I started asking everyone I bumped into if he or she had seen Mike Corby. Nobody had. Several said Cruz had asked them the same question earlier. I checked, and he wasn't in his room. Jennifer Schwartz didn't know where he was and was upset that he'd disappeared without making a notation in the sign-out log. I tried the motor pool and learned that Mike had taken one of the jeeps earlier in the day. You're supposed to enter your destination on the ticket when you do this, but this procedure (to Jennifer's despair) had always been loose and Mike had neglected to make the entry.

I went to the Blue Pigeon, where Meredy was tending bar. It was too early for the crowd, and she was free to talk. I bellied up and ordered a Carta Blanca.

"You heard about Cruz looking for Mike?"

Meredy nodded. "It's all over town. I tried to get to him, and warn him."

"Then you don't know where he is?"

"Haven't the faintest."

"Can Cruz really put him in the pokey for a little thing like that?"

"Out here in Chirapulco, Cruz can do pretty much what he wants. I suppose a lawyer could spring Mike easily enough, but it would take time. And in that time, Cruz would have made his point. Mike's dealing with Mexican pride here—the blood of the conquistadores and all that—and it's a powerful thing."

"We can't finish the picture without Mike," I said. "How long do you think we'd have to wait to get him back?"

"The bureaucratic wheels grind slowly here," she said sadly. "I can't say for sure, but it might be a matter of weeks."

I groaned—at least, inwardly. "We can't wait it out. Not unless Fargo comes up with a big hunk of immediate cash, and I don't think he's in the mood for that. Look, you've been working with Mike on all that filing business—he must have said something. He must have given you some indication of where he might disappear to."

Meredy shook her head. "He didn't say anything along those lines. He never even told me who he thinks the murderer is. Frankly, I don't believe he knows, in spite of what he said at the press conference. He was just taking a wild shot, I think, hoping to flush out the murderer."

I sipped the beer, which I didn't really want, but which gave me something to do with my hands. An actor always likes to have something to do with his hands. "I've got a sickening thought," I said. "Mike pointed out a pattern in these murders when we were talking it over. Everybody who got knocked off was having what used to be called an illicit love affair. Going off and shacking up with somebody else—secretly, for the most part. This applies to Mike himself. Do you suppose—" I shook my head abruptly. "Hell, no," I said, "it couldn't be anything like that."

Meredy's eyes widened. "You mean you think the murderer's kidnapped Mike, or something, and wants to kill him, too?"

"That's too far-out," I said, shrugging.

"I don't think it is," said Meredy slowly. "The whole thing's been far-out, right from the beginning. George, Mike *might* be in danger."

"He can take care of himself."

"So you think and so he thinks, I'm sure. But this is Mexico, George, and, believe me, I know, taking care of yourself's a lot more difficult here."

"Anyway, I've got to find Mike. Maybe there's some way I can spirit him out to the set and shoot that one scene before Cruz can get to him. But where the hell could he be? There's no place to go from here. The nearest town of any size is hours away over roads that would bog down a tractor. My posterior is still aching from the way we used to ride out to the—"

I stopped short.

"Are you all right?" asked Meredy.

I realized I'd been staring at her. "I'm okay," I said. "I think I know where Mike is. The best guess, anyway.

These love trysts I've been talking about. He said several of them took place in the old monastery. They have people out there—it's practically a village. He could have gone out there to talk to them—dig up leads or evidence. In fact, now that I think of it, it's about the only place he *could* have gone without disappearing for days."

"Then let's go find him!" said Meredy excitedly. "I can get off from work, just this once, I'm sure."

"You stay here. I'll find him."

"George—please. I happen to be in love with Mike. My God, did you hear what I just said? I haven't even said it to *him*, yet. Anyway, I've got to know if he's safe."

After a short frown, I said, "Well, okay, you can come along, if you want. Bring a jacket. You might need it up there."

"Up where?"

"I'm taking my airplane," I said. "I'm not going to beat up my kidneys riding out there one more time."

CHAPTER FIFTEEN

Many weeks before, when we were shooting at the old monastery, I'd had the notion of flying to the location area instead of jolting for a couple of hours over the adobe washboard that was the road. I'd checked the terrain and knew that there was a good, flat stretch of desert a short distance from the ruins where, with a little extra care, I could land safely. The Cessna, as I think I've mentioned, is equipped with Robertson STOL gear—the initials stand for Short Take Off and Landing—and I won't get into its technical aspects, but it means that I can drop it in between two cactus plants when I want to. As it happened, getting from the hotel to the airport and then readying the airplane turned out to be too complicated for the early morning, so I rode on bouncing wheels, along with everybody else. But I'd already made the short hop mentally.

There was a big, fat moon in an absolutely clear sky this evening. Getting down without runway lights would be no insurmountable problem. Meredy belted herself into the right-hand seat, I got a clearance in fairly intelligible English from the tower, and we were on our way.

Within minutes after takeoff, the old monastery was in sight. Nestled against a line of sawtooth hills that rose from the desert floor, it looked like a model of what it was. I banked so that Meredy could see it more clearly.

"San Ysidro," I said. "Built in the sixteenth century with Indian labor. One of the monastic orders used it as a retreat for a couple of centuries and then the irrigation water ran out, so they abandoned it. There's still water, though, from the springs in the hills—enough for a few squatters who live here. Not in the monastery itself—there's some superstition about that, apparently—but in their own shacks nearby. From time to time they think of turning it into a tourist attraction, but it's too far off the beaten track."

"Yes," said Meredy, without a great deal of interest in what I was saying. "I hope Mike's there."

I took one more look at the gloomy, crumbling walls and towers of the rambling structure, then flew a low box-pattern a little beyond it, over the patch of land I meant to set down upon. Everything looked clear; I lined up on final approach and coasted in. The landing was gentle, and I was pleased with it. Meredy, who made no comment, probably thought all landings on the desert at night went that easily.

I taxied back to a point as near the monastery as possible, and then we got out and walked. If any persons in the squatters' shacks had noticed us, they had not shown themselves, and that, I supposed, was to be expected; any news from the outside for these people was usually bad news; they lived in constant fear of being evicted.

The old structure loomed, dark and weird, on its little knoll just ahead of us. It had once been a lovely colonial edifice, with saints and angels carved into its sandstone facings, but now it was like something in a Salvador Dali painting. Inside, I knew, was a rabbit warren of rooms and corridors and a maze of courtyards; restored, the entire complex would have made an attractive resort hotel. When we had filmed a long sequence here, earlier, the construction gang had cleaned up several of the rooms and made them habitable so that, on occasion, members of the company could stay over and avoid the long trips to and from Chirapulco.

Walking upslope, Meredy and I were almost upon the monastery when we saw, parked near the crumbling walls, the jeep Mike had checked out of the motor pool. I hadn't noticed it from the air. We glanced inside and saw little more than the dusty seats.

"Where's Mike?" asked Meredy, frowning, looking in several directions. "If he heard the airplane, he'd come out to meet us, wouldn't he?"

I shrugged. "Maybe. But maybe not." That wasn't much of an answer, but it seemed to calm her down a little.

We continued toward the walls, and presently reached a large aperture that had once been an archway. As we were about to step into the shadows behind it, Mike stepped out of them, startling us and making Meredy gasp.

"*There* you are!" she said. "We were getting worried!"

Instead of looking happy to see us, Mike was scowling like a middleweight trying to psych his opponent as the referee gives instructions. "Listen, you two," he said, "get back in that plane and fly away again, will you?"

"After we took the trouble to come out here?" I returned Mike's scowl. "What the hell are you up to, anyway?"

"Can't tell you now," said Mike. "Just that you're in the way. How did you know I was here?"

"Guessed. After what you told me about all the rendezvous out here. Besides, it was about the only place you could have gone. We had to find you to warn you."

"About what?"

Meredy answered. "Cruz is looking for you. He wants to put you in jail. He's muttering things about withholding evidence and how, in his book, it's worse than stealing from nice old ladies."

"Damn!" said Mike. "That's all I need—for Cruz to show up now and ruin everything!"

"He may not show up," I said. "I don't think he knows you came here, though I suppose he could find out sooner or later, the same as we did. But, as it happens, Mike, I need you a lot more than Cruz does—to finish up those scenes. What I want to do is sneak you back to the set, hide you somewhere, and take a chance that Cruz won't put the arm on you till we're finished shooting."

Mike was thoughtful for a moment. "All that may not be necessary. If what I have in mind works out, Cruz ought to be satisfied and get off our backs once and for all."

For the first time I noticed that Mike had a revolver tucked into his belt; it looked like a snub-nosed Detective Special, the kind he was undoubtedly used to. The Property department had revolvers Mike could have acquired in some underhanded fashion, and in Mexico you can buy bullets in practically any corner drugstore, but I had an idea Mike had rat-holed this weapon away all this time simply because, as an ex-cop, he felt comfortable owning it and was willing to risk smuggling it into Mexico. All that was almost beside the point; what mattered was that he had the damn thing. I said, "Exactly what *do* you have in mind?"

"If I tell you, will you both get the hell out of here?"

"If that seems the thing to do."

"Okay," said Mike. "I'm only going to say this once, so listen. You both know how we put things together and learned that the monastery was serving as a love nest. We got all the combinations except Lance Haverford and his unknown partner. Now, exactly who was sleeping with whom may or may not mean anything, but in any case the list has to be complete. All the data has to be in before you even start thinking about it—no holes left unplugged. So that's the first reason I came here—to find out if any of the squatters got a look at any of the overnight visitors and could give me a description."

"And did they?"

"My Puerto Rican Spanish isn't exactly the same as theirs," said Mike, "and besides it doesn't remember itself too good. But we communicated, after a fashion. A couple of them remembered Lance. And could describe who was with him."

"Well, who was it?"

"I'm not going to say right now. If it turns out to be significant, you'll find out later. So it may or may not have been worthwhile, talking to those squatters. But

I've still got my second reason for coming here—and that's the main reason."

"Mike, you're not making sense—"

"I will, if you stop interrupting. At the press conference I hinted I knew who the guilty party was—said I was waiting for a confession. I could see that a lot of them didn't believe that, and they were absolutely right. But they don't know *for sure* whether or not I'm bluffing. That includes the murderer. And it means the murderer has to make a play. Get rid of me. No other choice. That's why I'm here, where it's remote and isolated. It's just too good a chance for the murderer to pass up."

"How do you know he'll find you here?" I asked.

"You found me, didn't you? I couldn't make the trail too obvious, or it would smell like a trap."

"This is crazy, Mike," I said. "Too many ifs and maybes in it. I still can't understand why someone would murder a whole bunch of people just because they'd been sleeping with each other."

Mike took in a deep breath to contain his impatience. "Murder out of moral indignation is more common than you think, especially with a flaked-out mind. It was Jack the Ripper's motive when he knocked off all those prostitutes in London. But it may be—it just may be—that there's an entirely different motive here."

"Okay. What?"

"Try to follow this now. You zero in on any unknown murderer through connections with the victim. The exception is when some nut goes out and kills a string of complete strangers. The Boston Strangler, Son of Sam, the Hillside Strangler, all those classic cases. Now, what if *our* killer only wanted to kill one person, but realized that a connection might be made? So instead, there's a whole list of victims—none of the others connected with the killer—as a smoke screen. The original motive gets lost and, even if it becomes evident, is disregarded because it doesn't match all the other murders!"

"Mike," said Meredy earnestly, "all this reverse-English is very intriguing, but don't you think it would be better if you just come back with us and try to finish those scenes tomorrow before Cruz finds you?"

He shook his head. "No, I'm staying here. And you two have to go back. Three's a crowd, and I don't think the murderer will make a play in a crowd."

She put her hands on Mike's arms and searched his eyes. "You think the murderer might make an attempt on *you*. What if that attempt succeeds?"

"Not likely," said Mike "The other victims weren't looking for it. I am." He patted the revolver thrust into his belt.

I said, "Where did you get that thing, anyway?"

"Property. They've got a regular arsenal. And you can buy real bullets instead of blanks anywhere in town. Now, stop asking questions and go on back, will you?"

Meredy put her palms to his cheeks and kissed his lips briefly. "Don't do it, Mike. Don't take even this chance. I waited a long time to get lucky and find you, and I don't want to lose you now."

He smiled a little. "Are we going to have our first quarrel?"

"Better than having our last," said Meredy.

Before anybody could say anything else—or think about anything else—there was the sound of a shot.

I flinched and ducked instinctively.

Two more shots sounded.

I heard a bullet hit somewhere in our general vicinity and then go screaming off in ricochet.

Mike and Meredy had also ducked. He had jerked her to one side, slammed her to the ground, then rolled over her to protect her with his body. From my own position—sprawled on my stomach a few feet from them—I stared in the direction from which the shots had come. As nearly as I could make out, the point of origin had been in the belfry of a tower that loomed skyward a little more than a hundred yards away from us. In the shadow of that belfry, and only for an instant, I thought I saw the movement of what looked like a rifle barrel being drawn back and out of sight.

"Mike . . ." said Meredy—her voice seemed oddly small and tight—"Mike . . . I think I'm hit—"

"Oh, no!" Mike pushed himself aside enough to look at her, then immediately placed his palm on the rump of her blue jeans and took it away again. In the moonlight, I saw the blood. He examined the spot more closely. "It's a gouge—a flesh wound—"

"It's starting to hurt. I don't think I can walk."

Another shot rang out and kicked up a spurt of dust about six feet beyond us. I flinched again. I wish I could say I bore up under it heroically and didn't so much as twitch a muscle. No, on second thought, I don't wish that. That would have been plain stupid—

"George, listen!" said Mike. He had his revolver in his hand now. "I'll suppress the fire up there. You drag Meredy back behind the wall. Fast as you can."

It was a good thing I was slightly numb from being shot at. It kept me from wondering how much of a better target I'd make, getting to my feet and pulling Meredy away from this open spot. This was no time for analysis or introspection, and when Mike pressed the button I went, unthinkingly, into action. Somehow, I got to my feet, leaned over, helped Meredy to a standing position, and then, with my arm around her waist and her arm around my shoulders, I stumbled forward with her to the archway from which Mike had emerged. At the same time, Mike rose to a crouch, and, steadying his gun with both hands, squeezed off three shots toward the tower.

There were no answering shots, but the lump of fear I'd suddenly developed about where my Adam's apple should have been stayed with me all the way to the shadows. When we reached this place of partial concealment, I lowered Meredy to the ground again, then squatted down beside her and removed my shirt to tear it into bandages.

Mike scuttled toward us. There was one more shot from the tower, and this time I saw the flash. He dove forward like a runner sliding headfirst into second and fetched up beside us.

When he'd picked himself up again, he glanced at the wound in Meredy's left buttock. "How is it?"

I was applying a strip of torn shirt. "I don't think the bullet's in there—"

"It hurts like hell!" said Meredy.

Mike nodded as though that were beside the point, and, under the circumstances, it probably was. "Now, look," he said. "You two stay here. Keep covered and don't budge. I'm going after that sniper."

"With that?" I looked at the revolver in his hand. He had taken a box of cartridges from his pocket, and was replacing the three empty shells. "It's no good at long range—I know that much about it—"

"Nothing else we can do," Mike said quickly, snapping the cylinder into place again. "We can't make it to the jeep or plane without getting shot. The only chance is for me to shortstop whoever's shooting at us."

"Yeah? And what do we do if you don't?"

"Run like hell," said Mike, "and say a prayer if you know one."

Weapon in hand, Mike broke away from us, and, staying in a crouch, ran zigzag through the rubble and toward the tower. I caught glimpses of him as he passed in and out of areas of shadow. There were two more shots from the tower as he crossed open spaces. Evidently he wasn't hit; he kept going.

Moments later, he was hunkered down behind a tall, eroded pillar that looked like a stalagmite growing from the floor of some weirdly lighted cave. All around him, the jagged shapes of the ruins formed stark patterns in the morbid, adipose sheen of the moonlight—it was like something a set designer with a bizarre turn of mind might have cooked up for the background of a terrifying dream sequence.

From our position, we could see the archways of the belfry, high in the tower, and we could see Mike squatting behind the pillar across from the tower, so that the line of fire between the belfry and Mike formed a hypoteneuse of—I don't know—maybe a hundred feet. It was evident that Mike and whoever was in the tower couldn't see each other unless they exposed themselves.

Then we heard Mike's voice, as he raised it to call up to the tower. "Can you hear me up there?"

The answer was a shot. Chips flew from the side of the column where Mike crouched. Watching him, I was glad to see that I wasn't the only one who flinched when getting shot at.

"Let's work this thing out!" Mike called. "Throw that gun down, and we'll talk it over! You want to explain everything—right? Okay; I'm ready to listen!"

There was a stretch of silence instead of a shot this time. I supposed the sniper up there in the tower was thinking over what Mike had said. I could detect the psychology in it—right out of seminars about what to do in situations like this—and I had the feeling that whoever was in that belfry could see through it as well as I could. But it had to be tried, of course. Anything and everything had to be tried.

Mike allowed the pause to hang for a few minutes, then called out again. "I know you've got troubles—we all have! This isn't the way to handle them! You let me know what they are, and I'll see what I can do. You won't be hurt—I can promise you that much!"

Another long silence. I squinted hard at the dark patch up there in the tower, but saw no movement. It occurred to me that the sniper, instead of thinking about Mike's remarks, was just holding that rifle ready, waiting for Mike to show himself.

"Think it over!" called Mike. "We can stay here all night like this—but that doesn't solve anything! Let's see what we can do about those problems of yours! Get rid of that gun, and let's talk, okay?"

I wasn't sure how long the next pause lasted. There were pulse-beats in my ears, but I wasn't counting them. The silence stretched out like a rubber band about to break. In the tension of these moments my sense of time was out of kilter and I couldn't tell whether minutes or seconds had passed since Mike had taken his position at the base of the tower.

There was movement in the shadows that cloaked a pile of rubble behind Meredy and myself. Maybe I saw it from the corner of my eye, or maybe I detected it through some gland in the back of my skull left over from the dinosaurs. I know that I was startled and snapped my head around and looked.

Someone stocky—someone in a cowboy costume of the kind they pass out to the extras—stood perhaps twenty feet away, partly in gloom, holding a rifle, waist-high, pointed directly at us.

I blinked at this apparition. In the time it took to blink, I realized what must have happened. Somehow, while Mike was reciting from the manual of how to get snipers to throw down their guns, this sniper had slipped away, descended from the tower, and circled around behind us.

The sniper took a step forward. This brought a little more light on the face under the brim of that dirty hat. I recognized that face.

"Phyllis!"

Phyllis Upton it was. She didn't answer. Instead of looking at me, she looked past me, with a strange, wooden expression I'd never seen on her face before. There was a curious flatness to her eyes—the zombie look some alcoholics take on as they approach a stupor. But I doubted that she was drunk. She was holding that rifle much too steadily to be drunk.

At last she spoke. Instead of the mellow voice I had known, something with reedy, strident undertones came out—almost the voice of another person. She was not addressing Meredy or myself, but calling to Mike, where he was squatting.

"Drop your gun! Try anything, and these two get it!"

I turned to look at Mike and saw him move slowly and reluctantly as he came to an understanding of what had happened. He tossed the gun to the ground in front of him, then rose and stepped away from the pillar.

"Phyllis?" He made a question out of it, though he knew very well it was she. "Hey! Phyllis! Come on, now—take it easy!"

"Shut up!" she said. "Come this way. Slowly. No tricks!"

He started walking. "Okay, Phyl. You do the talking. That's what you want, right? Somebody to listen? Somebody to understand?"

"Don't give me that bullshit!" she said. "You're like all the rest!"

It wasn't Phyllis Upton talking, I was thinking. It was the other half of a personality split right down the middle. It was Phyllis Upton spelled backwards. I can't pronounce Phyllis Upton spelled backwards, and, in the same way, I couldn't quite put her together even as I stared at her. That rigid expression on her face and those dead-fish eyes intensified her warthog ugliness—

"No, Phyl, I'm not like all the rest," said Mike, still approaching slowly. "Neither are George and Meredy here. We're your friends. You don't need that gun. Put it down, okay?"

She did not move the rifle but both her voice and her expression seemed to soften a little as she said, "Why did you have to do this, Mike? Why did you have to bring these two into it?"

"Just the way everything worked out. I thought it might be you. I wasn't sure, but when I heard about you and Lance—"

"Stop right there!" said Phyllis.

Mike came to a halt. His face was so calm as to be expressionless. He couldn't be that calm inside, I thought. Nobody could. It was something he had taught himself.

"Why don't you tell us about it?" he said. "Get it off your chest."

"What the hell difference does it make now?" There was what I thought might be a faint note of anguish in Phyllis's voice.

"You want us to know why, don't you? I've guessed

200

some of it, but not all. I won't really understand until I hear everything."

"Smart ass," said Phyllis. The side of her personality she was showing now was a lot coarser than the side we'd known. Maybe that's true, to a degree, of everybody. It's like reading a book on abnormal psychology and realizing, with a shock, that you've got a little of everything in it. "What do you know? Or think you know?"

"You really only wanted to kill one person, right? The others were a smoke screen—"

"Maybe. But they had it coming to them."

"How do you figure that, Phyllis?"

"It's none of your fucking business," she said.

"I suppose not," said Mike. I could sense some of the technique he was employing. The one thing you don't do with a nut who has a gun pointed at you, the manual must have said, is contradict him. "But you must have had some kind of justification. I just want to know what it is."

"Lance," she said, her eyes shifting queerly. "The sonofabitch. He *had* to die. I don't know why I believed him! All his talk about beauty being only skin deep! He said—" she drew a deep breath— "he said he loved me!"

Mike nodded. "I knew you and Lance had been making it together, though I didn't find that out till tonight, when I talked to those squatters—"

She went on as though Mike hadn't spoken. "It was some kind of joke with him! He couldn't keep his hands off anybody! Not even me—and I know what I am! I've had to live with it all my life, and I never kidded myself about it! That shrink I went to used to say it wasn't enough to worry about, but he didn't know his ass from a hole in the ground! Nobody knows! Nobody knows what it is when you can't get anybody even to make love to you!"

"Lance did, didn't he?" Mike said gently.

"Yes. He went through the whole act—the whole goddamn ritual of seduction! And all the time he was laughing at me. Do you know what he said after I gave

201

him what he wanted? *He said he always wanted to know what it would be like to make love to a really ugly woman!*"

"Phyl," said Mike, "that's all over with now. You can relax. You don't have to trouble yourself with a lot of planning—a lot of worry about who's going to find out. So put down the gun—"

"Like hell!" she said. She moved the gun a little as though to remind Mike that it was still there, though none of us needed much reminding. "You said you wanted to know everything. All right—I'm telling you. You're right about the others; they had to go so all the attention wouldn't be on Lance—and then on me when they found out about us. But you see what they were, and why they had to die, don't you? They were just like Lance! The beautiful people! That's what they're called, you know! And they don't have any real love for anybody—only themselves! Trish, Wally, Joel, even that bullfighter—though he knew too much—"

"We understand, Phyl. Take it easy."

"No, you don't understand everything. How they all thought I was never one of them—thought I was too stupid to do anything about it! But I outsmarted them all the way. I made a list. Lance was neither first nor last— nobody ever knew he was the main one who had to be killed—"

"That doesn't matter now, Phyl. It's all over."

"Not yet!" she said. Her eyes shifted as she looked at Meredy, and then at me, and then at Mike again. "I don't like doing this. But you're the only ones who know now."

"Phyl, you've already made your point," said Mike, taking a cautious step forward. "You've proved everything you wanted to prove—even that you could bring the picture in, where Lance probably would have failed. We were never on your list, Phyl, and we're not on it now. We're not beautiful people. We're like you, Phyllis, doing the best we can with what we've got—"

I don't know whether it was what Mike said or the way he said it that had what was almost a hypnotic effect on Phyllis. I'm sure that with that little black hole at the end of that rifle staring at me I couldn't have thought of the words he was finding, nor could I have delivered them in such a calm and soothing tone of voice. In a way, Mike was giving me a hell of a lesson in acting, which means making your voice and your whole body, even your central nervous system, do exactly as you wish it to do, anyplace, anytime.

"I won't lie to you, Phyllis," he said, still moving slowly toward her. "We can't agree with what you've done—we're shocked by it, same as everybody else. But I think we understand. I think we can see how the pressure got to be just too much to bear—"

He leapt forward. There must have been a microsecond in which he prepared himself for that movement, but I didn't see it and neither did Phyllis. His whole body moved as swiftly as Glenn Ford's hand in a fast draw; he was nothing but a blur as he hurled himself at her. In one moment he was facing her across a distance of several feet; in the next he was upon her, grabbing the barrel of the rifle and swinging it upward and outward, away from all of us.

The rifle went off. A spurt of orange flame speared itself up into the night, and the blast, so near to us now, was sharp and close to painful in my eardrums. The smell of the burnt explosive was bitter in my nostrils.

Mike twisted hard, wrenched the weapon out of Phyllis's grasp, and tossed it aside.

She stared at him as though she didn't believe he was there. She stared at him for one frozen moment, and then suddenly she brought her hands to her face and began to sob.

Mike sighed, stepped back, and just stood there, looking at her. I didn't know what he was thinking. I didn't know what I was thinking.

We weren't thinking—any of us. Not me, not Mike, not Meredy. Not Phyllis. It was a moment that had numbed all of our thoughts and a moment I knew I never wanted to relive, not even in a dream. . . .

CHAPTER SIXTEEN

As I've said, I'm not big on parties, but this one, shortly after Award night, was in honor of all the Oscars *The Godless* had won. Best screenplay, best photography, best music, best costumes—a bevy of bests right down the line. The award for best director was given to Joel Totterelli posthumously, and Roberta Vale received best supporting actress the same way.

Drink in hand—a plain ginger ale because I wasn't in the mood for anything stronger—I picked my way through the jam-packed conversational groups to find a quiet corner, returning greetings and smiling and nodding when I had to.

"George," said Francis Coppola as I passed—he was between beards and I almost didn't recognize him—"you should have at least gotten credit for a save, like a relief pitcher in the ninth."

"Thanks, Francis," I said. "I'm just glad the whole project finally got off the ground."

The party was in the biggest and fanciest banquet room of the biggest and fanciest hotel J. Sutton Fargo could find. He had invited everyone who had had any connection with the picture; Marilou Fargo had added to the guest list everyone she'd always wanted to meet.

Everybody who came brought at least two cousins, twice removed. Add to this the usual gate-crashers and a squad of paparazzi with their Nikons, and you've got the milling gaggle it turned out to be.

I elbowed past Fargo, who, wearing a quiet tux, was bending the ears of Burt Reynolds, who had Blossom Foster on his arm. Cameras were clicking and I knew the gossip media would be linking Burt romantically with the woman they were already calling the newest sex kitten on the Hollywood scene. The link didn't look romantic to me, but I supposed the publicity wouldn't hurt *The Godless*, which was already breaking box-office records.

"Yes, sir!" Fargo was saying. "Even when everything looked like it was lost, I never once lost faith in the picture! It was somethin' America needed, and, by God, I was determined to give it to 'em!"

"Uh huh," said Burt politely.

Blossom Foster giggled.

My progress took me past Jennifer Schwartz and Ira Yoder in a corner. Separated only by the swelling of her bazooms, they were staring soulfully into each other's eyes. That *did* look like a romantic link to me, but none of the paparazzi knew who they were.

At last I found a cul-de-sac with a sofa and a television set. I grabbed a couple of canapés from a passing tray and sat down. No sooner had I done so, than Mike Corby, rolling along like a bandy-legged bulldog, squeezed himself out of the crowd and sat down beside me.

"Some party," said Mike.

"Yeah," I said.

I could see we were about to enter into a regular fugue of brilliant dialogue again.

"Meredy's with Vincent Price," he said, nodding toward the crowd, which was too dense for either of us to see through. "They're talking about her paintings. I can't understand half of it. They must be okay, though— she's still selling a few. And where we are, in Albuquerque, she's turning them out like hotcakes. I guess she thrives on the peace and quiet there."

"Everything okay now on those charges?" I asked.

"Just like the lawyers said. Probation. They even gave her permission to move out of the state so I could take the job at the university. Expensive as hell, but I could finally afford it and it was worth it."

"Good," I said.

"Yeah," said Mike. He leaned back, glass of champagne in hand, and looked thoughtful. "Know what? I miss Phyllis."

"I kind of do too," I said, frowning.

"The murders were sickening, and she was sick—and it was all rotten and shocking—but in some stupid way I wish she could be here, enjoying all this success with the rest of us."

"I saw Phyllis at the hospital," I said. "It was pretty good of the Mexicans to let her be transferred there, back to her own country. She didn't recognize me. She doesn't recognize anybody. Just stares at nothing all day and mutters in a voice like a little girl. I keep wondering where the justice is in any of this."

"There ain't no justice," said Mike. "Ask anybody in the business."

I looked at my watch. "Revelstoke's on in a minute. I understand he's going to say something about *The Godless*."

Mike shrugged. "Get a couple of airsick bags and we'll listen."

I leaned forward and switched the set on. Revelstoke, sitting behind his desk, and with the chromo screen in back of him, faded in on the tube.

"Good evening one and all!" he said smugly. "I have exclusive information that, because of the success of *The Godless*, all major studios and networks are now planning to produce westerns and that we are about to see a return of this once-popular genre.

"Let us look at this genre for a moment. It is the basic American morality play. In it, we are shown that, in the end, the good guys always win and the bad guys always get what's coming to them. But I have news for you, dear friends. It's not at all like that in real life, and, indeed, sometimes it is quite the opposite.

"In furthering this myth, Hollywood disarms us as we face a dangerous world, and therefore does us a great disservice. They show us life, not as it really is, but as we wish it could be. This is not truth, and therefore it is not art. I am appalled to see a resurgence of the western, or any other category that uses similarly predictable clichés—"

"Turn him off!" groaned Mike.

"Right." I reached out and did so.

Mike jiggled the champagne in his glass without tasting it. "But the sonofabitch is right, at that," he said. "The bad guys *don't* always get their just deserts. Revelstoke himself. When he reported all that inside stuff on the murders, he got bigger than ever. And Alfonso Cruz. He got credit for the collar and they shipped him to Mexico City and promoted him to *comisario*—the same as inspector."

"Was he a bad guy?"

"To me, he was. Though not altogether. I guess none of the bad guys were altogether bad. But you see what I mean."

"Not really."

"Okay, take the good guys. Me. I thought, when I paid off my debts, married Meredy, and settled down in Albuquerque, I'd live happily ever after."

"Isn't that what you're doing?"

"You don't know how it is, George," he said, corrugating his forehead and most of the battered countenance below it. "Dull as hell, nothing happening. The only crime they have is petty and sordid, and all that sunshine, day after day—a goddamn bore, and not a decent delicatessen in town. I'd like to go back to NYPD but they're still sore at me for quitting and becoming an actor. God, how I crave those dirty streets I used to walk! You know something? I'm miserable!"

I got up.

"Where are you going?"

"Mike," I said, looking down at him, "this is where I came in."

THE END

FLANAGAN'S RUN

TOM McNAB

The first and only Trans-America Race: 3,000 miles for $300,000. The press called Flanagan's race impossible. Crazy! But as Depression America cheered, two thousand hopefuls left Los Angeles running for New York City and their wildest dreams of riches!

Fifty miles a day. Day after day. It took more than raw courage. Five runners—a beautiful dancer and four determined men—pushed beyond physical exhaustion to the sheer exhilaration of a superhuman challenge. Until the miles became days, the pain became pure spirit, and their hearts became one in the magnificent drive for victory! 63149-0/$3.95

Tom McNab was Script Consultant/Technical Adviser of CHARIOTS OF FIRE

SELECTED BY THE LITERARY GUILD AND READER'S DIGEST CONDENSED BOOKS

Available wherever paperbacks are sold or directly from the publisher. Include 50¢ per copy for postage and handling: allow 6-8 weeks for delivery. Avon Books, Mail Order Dept., 224 W. 57th St., N.Y., N.Y. 10019

Flanagan 3-83